REVIVAL

Revival

A Bella James Mystery

Alexis Koetting

Copyright © 2020 Alexis Koetting

Editor: Mary Ann J. Blair
Front cover image: Shutterstock/Nicole Dericks
Grunge background by Nik Merkulov/Shutterstock.com
Author photo: Sally LeDrew
Cover design: Ruth Dwight
Issued in print and electronic formats.
ISBN (paperback): 978-1-7774423-0-9
ISBN (EPUB): 978-1-7774423-1-6

This is an original print edition of Revival.

*For Tom, who is experiencing a
revival of his own.*

The word revival *refers to the restoration of a being to life, consciousness, vigour, or strength.*

In the theatre, it is a term for a new production of an old play.

Chapter 1

"What's that sound?"

"I don't hear anything."

"Shhh," I said.

"It's a little hard to be quiet when there's—"

"Shhh," I said again.

I was at a drive-in movie with Paul, my fella of almost two years. There were four screens, two of which currently had movies playing. Our first film had finished and we were in the middle of the intermission that divided the double feature.

It was rare for me to have a night off on the weekend. The two shows I was performing in at the Shaw Festival had been programmed with one or the other playing most Friday and Saturday evenings. Paul and I were, happily, still in that stage of our relationship where we made time for dates, so we took full advantage when gifted with an evening that didn't precede an early morning at the animal hospital where Paul worked as a vet.

It was a warm night. A welcome, although I feared brief, respite from the sweltering summer temperatures. With the sound coming through the cars' stereo systems, many people had their windows open or had opted to bring lawn chairs to sit outside, so there were odd moments when a meandering car chase or shoot out collided with the boy and girl finally realizing they're in love on the neighbouring screen. That, combined with parents rushing excited children to the bathrooms, car doors slamming, and the teenage boys talking extra loudly in a desperate attempt to drown out the clanging of their contraband beer bottles, made my request for silence almost laughable.

I'd never been to a drive-in before. There was one on Prince Edward Island, where I grew up, but I'd never had any friends to go with nor the inclination to do anything that might put a smile on my face. I looked around now at all the laughing high-school students spilling out of cars to refill their drinks and snacks before the next movie. Some were obviously on dates. Some were looking to get dates. Regardless, they were all having fun. Made me wonder how different my childhood would have been if I'd known how to do that.

"I used to come here all the time," Paul said. "Me and my friend Dan. We'd take turns hiding in the trunk."

"Why? So you wouldn't have to pay?"

"No. It made us look really cool in front of our dates."

I laughed out loud, waking Moustache, an oodle of some sort and the canine owner of most of my heart. He'd been sleeping off a popcorn coma in the back seat but woke with a second wind, climbed into my lap, and dove his furry beige face into the empty popcorn container that had been discarded at my feet.

"And just how many dates did you bring here?" I asked around the dog's rear end.

His tail brushed back and forth against my face.

"Oh, lots."

"Lots?"

"Sure. Not only was it a great place to make out, but it was a great place to be *seen* making out."

"What?"

"I'm serious! One's whole social standing could be made or broken based on—"

"There it is again! Did you hear that?"

I shifted Moustache to the back seat and got out of the car. I looked to where I thought the noise had come from, but all I could see were the fluorescent lights of the snack bar.

"It sounded like a … scream or a cry or something," I said, sticking my head in through the open window.

"It's probably just some kids goofing off."

"Maybe," I said.

But I wasn't convinced. I stood absolutely still, straining to hear that one sound amid all the noise.

"The movie's about to start," Paul said.

The screen showed a countdown and people hurried back to their cars, their arms loaded with hot dogs, candy, nachos. Moustache's gaze followed each one with open-mouthed anticipation and hope. I got back into the car just as the shriek came again. I looked at Paul.

"That?" he asked.

I nodded. Moustache sat upright with his head cocked.

"Sounds like a fox to me."

Fox sightings were common in the Niagara Region, especially in the more remote places. Moustache had been confounded by many.

"The mating cry often sounds like a scream," Paul said.

"Is this mating season?"

"Well, no. It's typically in the winter. But that doesn't mean there's not some randy fox out there trying to woo some special vixen."

"By luring her to the drive-in?"

"It's a romantic place," he said, sliding closer to me.

"Is that the move you used to win over Susie High School?"

"One of them," he said, as he leaned in to kiss me. "Want to see some of my others?"

I ran my fingers through his hair and pulled him closer to me.

The noise pierced the air once more. I broke the embrace. "That's no fox."

I was out of the car first. Paul was close behind. Moustache watched us through the rear window. I ran through a crowd of people as they returned to their cars and caught the end of a tray with my elbow. Popcorn and drinks fell to the ground. Choice words were yelled at my back. I muttered an apology but didn't stop.

We were by the entrance to the concessions area. The noise was closer but growing faint. The incessant popping of the popcorn maker thundered in my ears making the noise's direction hard to place. No one else seemed to hear anything out of the ordinary and, had Paul not been ten feet away from me straining his ears, I'd have thought I was going crazy.

"This way," he said and darted around the corner of the building.

I followed and almost ran into his back where he had stopped.

There were five dumpsters lined up against the outer wall of the snack bar. All had been tagged by amateur graffiti artists and three were full. The mounds of black plastic bags looked like a mountain range. Some of the bags had been picked through by scavengers and their contents had slopped down the sides of the containers and spilled onto the ground. The pavement was sticky and littered with half-eaten food scraps, plastic lids with straws still attached, and soiled napkins. There was a sickly-sweet smell of rancid butter and ketchup.

And there was the sound.

"It might be a fox. Or a rat," Paul said. "I mean, look at this place, it's a smorgasbord for critters."

I shook my head and put my ear to the first dumpster.

"Could be an opossum," Paul continued.

"Shhh."

The first three dumpsters yielded nothing. I put my ear to the fourth, and my breath caught in my throat. I waved Paul over.

"It's in here. Whatever it is."

"Bells, I want you to stand over there behind that bin," he said, pointing to the last of the dumpsters.

"I want to help," I protested.

"Of the two of us, I'm the only one who's had a rabies shot. If anyone's going in there, it's me. You need to stand as far away as possible in case this thing shoots out of here. Which it likely will because I'm about to interrupt its supper, and I'm guessing it's going to be pissed."

"Paul, I don't think it's—"

"Bella, I need to believe I'm going to find an angry fox, okay? The alternative is…"

I nodded, and he heaved himself up and into the trash.

The sound became more intermittent and quieter than it had been.

The waiting was interminable.

"Bella," Paul finally called from inside the bin. "You need to call Jeffers."

Chapter 2

The baby didn't live long. And, by all accounts, he wouldn't have even if we'd found him sooner. He was severely deformed and obviously premature. The paramedics were surprised he'd lived as long as he did.

Paul had tried to resuscitate the baby and was still administering CPR when the ambulance arrived even though we both knew the little one was already gone. Paul hadn't spoken since the baby had been taken away.

Detective Sergeant Andre Jeffers had been first on the scene and had called in the necessary units after seeing what Paul and I had discovered. A member of the Major Crimes Unit of the Niagara Regional Police, Jeffers and I had formed a strong friendship after working on a couple of cases together—a sore spot for Paul and the cause of the only tension that existed between us. He didn't mind the friendship. He liked Jeffers. He didn't like me getting involved in potentially dangerous situations. I couldn't really blame him. Jeffers had saved my life twice.

"He going to be okay?" Jeffers asked, nodding to where Paul sat against the food-spattered wall with his eyes closed.

"Yeah," I said. "He's angry. Who would do something like this?"

"Normally, I'd say the baby's mother but…"

"Detective, we're ready," a white-clad man from the coroner's office said as he approached Jeffers' side.

Jeffers nodded.

"Bring her up," the man called to his colleagues.

Gently, the body of a woman was lifted out of the dumpster. She had been fitted with a body bag, and while I couldn't see the extent of her violation, I shuddered all the same.

"Paul said it looked like she'd been mutilated?"

"Could be a Caesarean gone wrong. I don't know. Won't know anything until the autopsy. Maybe not even then. Poor thing was a mess." Jeffers ran his hands through his hair and shook his head. "Dammit," he said quietly. "Times like these, I really hate my job."

"They'll figure it out. And then you'll find whoever did this. It's what you're best at," I said, giving Jeffers' arm a tender squeeze.

He patted my hand but didn't smile or seem at all comforted by my words. Not that I really expected him to. There's no comfort to be found in the murder of a baby only hours old. And certainly nothing to smile about in the carving up of a young woman.

"You guys should go," Jeffers said. "We're going to be here awhile."

"Do you want me to call Aria?" I asked, referring to Jeffers' wife.

"No. I'll do that. I could use the sound of her voice right about now."

I gave his arm another squeeze and moved toward Paul. He opened his eyes when I got near.

"Time to go," I said and held out my hand to him. He took it and raised himself up.

There was a small crowd on the other side of the police tape that blocked off the alley, along with news trucks from TV and radio stations. A woman in a red blazer asked a question and pushed a microphone in my direction. Paul swung his arm over my shoulder and steered me under the tape and away.

We arrived at the car to find Moustache fast asleep in the driver's seat.

"You mind driving?" Paul asked.

"Not at all," I said, as I scooped thirty pounds of sleeping dog into my arms. He woke and licked my face. He tried to squirm free, but I held him close, kissed the top of his fluffy head, and willed myself not to cry.

With our belts buckled and the dog hanging his head out of the back window, we joined the queue of cars leaving the grounds.

Police officers were looking into the vehicles and questioning people as they left.

"Evening, folks," one of them said when we'd pulled into position. "Oh! Emma! Bella, I mean. Ms. James!"

He had rested his hands on the window sill of the car door when he greeted us and quickly drew them away when he saw me behind the wheel, losing his footing when he did so and folding the side mirror when he tried to right himself.

I was known for playing Emma Samuel, a street-smart detective, on the popular police procedural *Port Authority*. Although the show had been off the air for a number of years, the fan base remained and often petitioned for a revival of the series. Or a movie at the very least. As far as I knew, there weren't plans for either.

Jeffers found it amusing to call me by my alter ego's name, as if by doing so he could make our past ventures more legitimate somehow. Paul, on the other hand, was frustrated by the blurred lines that existed between me and Emma and often had to remind me that playing at cops and robbers did not make me a real detective.

And then there were those who were simply star-struck upon meeting me. Or rather, Emma. I really didn't figure in. It was Emma Samuel they wanted to see.

I barely recognized the officer as the same one who had given me a ride home from the station years before. He had been completely overwhelmed by the assignment, and I remembered trying to relax him by telling him some behind-the-scenes stories. I seemed to recall the poor thing barely breathed for the duration of the drive. Then, he looked like a boy playing dress-up in his dad's uniform, but now he boasted a five o'clock shadow and biceps that strained the stitching of his sleeves.

"Bella is fine," I said, smiling.

"You can go on through, ma'am—Bella. Detective Sergeant Jeffers already gave the word."

I nodded my thanks.

Behind the officer, I could see television cameras being hefted onto shoulders and three reporters with microphones jockeying for position. The car's dashboard clock read 10:57. It was all too clear what the night's top story would be.

***

"I just saw you on the news," my best friend, Natalie, said over the phone.

Paul and I had left the drive-in less than an hour ago, and we were sitting in my living room nursing a Jack Daniels and a red wine, respectively.

"What happened?" she asked.

Natalie and I had met in our university days. Both of us were between roommates and were looking for someone with whom to share rent. Natalie had put an ad in the paper, promising a clean, safe, living space. And privacy. When I moved in with her, I had no intention of developing a friendship. For months, we each came and went on our own time, shared pleasant but brief conversations as we did dishes or exchanged places in the bathroom, and generally kept out of each other's way. Or rather, I kept out of her way. In time, we grew more comfortable with each other. More familiar. And before I knew it, and could keep it from happening, I'd made a friend. My first real one. One I couldn't imagine living without all these years later.

Paul excused himself and went into the kitchen, followed by a hopeful Moustache.

I told Natalie how we had come upon the grisly scene but, as the baby hadn't been mentioned in the news report, I left out that detail as well. I knew the police must have a reason for wanting that to remain confidential for the time being. Not that I didn't trust her. She had been privy to details of past cases I'd worked on with Jeffers. But I wasn't working on this one, and I felt it best to follow protocol.

"That's so cliché," she said when I'd finished.

"What?"

"I'm not trying to be unsympathetic but hiding a body in a dumpster never ends well."

It was true that dumpsters had long been the favoured place for the disposal of human remains. It was also true that the discovery of said remains was often inevitable.

What I hadn't told Natalie was that the victim had been stuffed into a tattered hockey bag that would have likely escaped notice going from dumpster to truck to trash compactor. What I didn't tell her was that if the zipper hadn't been broken, the cries of the newborn likely wouldn't have been noticed either.

We had a brief back-and-forth about our lives and jobs, and then I ended the call with a promise to trek to Toronto soon for one of our Chinatown feeding frenzies.

I found Paul sitting at the kitchen table, rubbing Moustache's ears with one hand and twirling a fresh glass of Jack Daniels in the other.

"I've witnessed the final moments of a lot of animals under a lot of different circumstances," Paul said. "But that baby…"

I joined him at the table. Moustache stretched out on the floor so that parts of him were in contact with parts of both of us. We sipped our drinks in a silence I was sure wouldn't last. Natalie hadn't been the only one tuned into the news, I was positive about that.

Chapter 3

There were two vans parked in front of the Royal George Theatre when I arrived for my matinee the following afternoon. When it was built in 1915, the theatre's purpose was to provide wartime entertainment for soldiers. Over the years, it transitioned through vaudeville to cinema to become the second largest of the three theatres that made up the Shaw Festival. Its modest red-and-white facade stood right on Niagara-on-the-Lake's main street and was blocked from view by the newshounds. I recognized one of the vans from the drive-in the night before. The colourful decals proudly, and loudly, advertised a local TV station. The other van bore the CBC News logo.

The sidewalks were conveyor belts of slow-moving tourists and, rather than do my usual high-speed weave through the crowd, I ducked my head, fell into step, and did my best to blend in.

The stage door was tucked away in an alley along the side of the theatre, and I slipped away from the cover of the masses, passed two ladies fanning themselves with programs, and hurried to the entrance. I had just sighed with relief when a young man with a mop of red hair stepped into my way with a microphone and a smile.

"Bella, you were at the Can-View Drive-In last night. Can you tell us what you saw?"

"The zombie love story," I said.

My unexpected response made him pause just enough to allow me to make my escape through the open stage door.

"I was keeping an eye out for you," Adam Lange said, as he pulled the door closed behind him.

Adam had been with the Shaw for several years before I joined the company and was easily becoming one of its stars. We had formed a fast and easy friendship almost immediately upon meeting two seasons prior and had been lucky to share shows ever since.

This year, he was playing my love interest in J.M. Barrie's *Quality Street*, which lent itself to all kinds of rehearsal awkwardness. Eventually, we worked through the giggling and the ickiness of having to look googly-eyed at someone you likened to a sibling and managed to generate a very sweet, very charming chemistry that reviewers, across the board, were applauding and audiences were rooting for.

"I know you're probably not allowed to talk about what happened, but I just want to know two things," Adam said, as we made our way down the stairs that led to the lounge area and dressing rooms. "First, are you okay?"

"Yes. I'm shaken but okay."

"Good. Next. Did you love the zombie movie?"

He had been the one to recommend the film despite a landslide of bad press.

"It was terrible! I never should have listened to you. That movie has no artistic merit whatsoever."

He put a hand to his heart, as if I'd wielded a mortal blow. "It most certainly does! And his name is Ashton Ryan. He has one of the best 'artistic merits' I've ever seen."

I laughed. "Don't tell that to Powell," I said, referring to his boyfriend of almost a year.

"Honey, who do you think dragged me to that piece of crap in the first place?"

We arrived at my dressing-room door. Adam had succeeded on two fronts: he'd saved me from the cameras and managed to put a smile on my face, the latter of which I'd been struggling with since the events of the night before.

"Do you need anything?" he asked. "I'm going to make a tea. I can bring you one."

"That gross throat stuff?"

"It's not gross."

"It smells gross."

"It works. I haven't had so much as a tickle in my throat for years."

"I'll take your word for it."

"All right. I'll see you out there, luvah," he said, giving my shoulder a rub and moving off down the hall.

"Thank you," I called after him.

He blew me a kiss then disappeared around a corner.

I stood in the doorway, staring at the wig of Regency curls that would transform me into Miss Phoebe Throssel, one of two sisters running a school for genteel children out of their home.

When we first meet Phoebe, she is convinced the dashing Captain Valentine Brown is set to propose. Instead, he tells her he's leaving to join the fight against Napoleon.

When he returns, ten years later, Phoebe, having let herself become an old maid, takes on the persona of a lively, flirtatious, and fictional niece, Livvy. Under this guise, she captivates not only Brown, but a number of other young men. Hilarity ensues, true love prevails, and the audience leaves smiling, having been treated to a few hours of frivolity.

It was not at all what I was in the mood for.

I shared the room with three other actresses, one of whom was stretched out on a yoga mat on the floor engaged in some deep breathing exercises. Margo Livingston played my sister in the play and we'd gotten to know each other quite well over the course of rehearsals. She had been blessed with a full figure, impeccable comic timing, and could teach a master class in the art of deadpan. Never a leading lady, Margo had made a career as a character actress and had taught me more than a thing or two in our time together.

I carefully stepped over her and made my way to my spot against the wall.

Our other two roommates hadn't yet arrived, and I was grateful for the silence. I had to get my head in the game. This production had become one of the season's surprise hits. Not only had the newspapers been extremely kind in their reviews, but it was a script that was rarely produced. The Shaw had dug it out of the annals of the British repertoire and dusted it off. And, in doing so, had introduced audiences to a whole new Barrie with nary a pirate nor a crocodile in sight. I imagined the keepers of his estate gleefully drinking tea while Peter Pan sulked in a corner with his shadow in his hand, refusing to grow up.

I tucked my hair under a wig cap and secured Phoebe's curls. I added liner to my eyes, pink to my cheeks, filled out my brows, and was just slipping into my petticoat when the two other actresses made their entrance. I greeted them with as much cheer as I could muster then shoved my earbuds into my ears and escaped into the hallway where I hoped my pre-show playlist would vanquish all thoughts of bodies and babies and blood.

"That's a nice look," Jeffers said when I emerged through the stage door three hours later.

Removing the wig cap was a hair lottery. Sometimes my long hair emerged in rather sexy waves; other times, its state would rival any rat's nest. Today it was a weird combination of the two.

"You look like Aden when he gets up from a nap after he's had a tantrum." Jeffers' toddler was in the midst of the terrible twos.

"A compliment will only get you so far," I said, digging into my purse for an elastic and whipping my hair into a ponytail. "What are you doing here?"

"I'm taking you for gelato."

We turned out of the alley onto the main street. The heat was oppressive and felt even hotter coming from the air-conditioned theatre. Even with sunglasses, the sun was harsh.

"I thought we were supposed to have a couple of cooler days," I said, as we made our way along Queen Street.

A few patrons recognized me from the play and called out congratulations. I was happy to see that the news trucks hadn't waited around.

"We are," Jeffers said. "It's three degrees cooler than it was yesterday. It was a whole ten minutes before I sweated through my shirt today rather than the usual six."

Il Gelato di Carlotta was packed. Inside and out. The *latteria* had opened several years earlier and boasted the best authentic Italian gelato in the region. I ordered a cup of the chocolate orange while Jeffers went for a waffle-cone combo of dark chocolate and tiramisu and, after a short walk, we were seated in the shade of a tree in Nelson Park overlooking the lake.

"So how are you doing?" Jeffers asked.

"What do you mean?"

"After last night. How are you doing?"

"Is that why you came all the way out here?"

"'All the way out here?' I work twenty minutes away."

"It's further than that."

"Bella, I don't want to debate distance with you. I want to know how you're doing."

"I'm fine," I said, spooning some gelato into my mouth.

"Really?"

I hesitated. "Yes."

Jeffers peered at me as if trying to see inside my brain. "How's Paul?"

"He's … less fine," I said, shuffling my position, more from being unnerved by Jeffers' intense gaze than because of any physical discomfort.

"We have people," Jeffers said. "At the office. A trauma team. They're trained to offer support after particularly difficult incidents. I just thought if you or Paul needed someone to talk to, I can certainly set something up."

"Jeffers, a man blew his head off in front of me. I think I know—"

"No, you don't know, Bella. You don't know!"

The last time Jeffers and I had worked together on a case, our killer had confessed in dramatic fashion just prior to taking his own life. I had unfortunately witnessed it.

I had also seen the accident photos of the crash that killed my parents. I had been eight when they died, and it was many years later that I went searching for details. The detectives had strongly advised me against it, but I'd insisted. And persisted.

There are things you can't unsee in life. Images that stay with you. That pass through your thoughts, called up by a reminder or as the result of a random shuffling of the brain's files. Whether they continued to haunt you or simply became a part of your history was up to you, I supposed. I treasured those pictures. To me they were totems of lives lived. Lives stolen. And reminders of the final breath that took them away to … peace.

I imagined this case stung Jeffers in a different way from most of the others because of the baby. Because he was a father. I ate the rest of my gelato in silence and waited for some of the tension to drop out of his shoulders before I spoke again.

"I'll let Paul know."

Jeffers nodded.

"Thank you."

He nodded again.

"I know I shouldn't ask, but do you have any idea who she was? Or is it too soon?"

"No, we got an ID right away," Jeffers said. "She was in the database. An MP."

"A missing person?"

"For six years. The family supplied DNA back then. All her information popped right up."

"Six years?"

"Likely a runaway based on what I read in her file. I'll know more once I've talked with the family."

"Her family," I said.

"What?"

"You keep saying 'the family.' She's a person, Jeffers. Regardless of what may have happened in her life, *she* had a family who has probably been through hell all these years. Wondering. Waiting. Blaming themselves. Someone cared enough to file a missing persons' report and that someone is *her* family. Not *the* family."

Jeffers side-eyed me and smirked. "Never thought you'd be one to wax poetic about family. You're getting soft, Samuel."

"Don't tell anybody," I said, giving him a playful punch in the arm.

I moved in with my father's mother after my parents died and proceeded to distance myself from anyone and everyone. Terri-Mae had endured years of glowering, morose, and sullen behaviour while I refused contact with my mother's parents and siblings. I left her house as soon as I was legally able, moved thousands of kilometres away, and would have never spoken to her again if it hadn't been for Natalie. Natalie had encouraged me to mend things with Terri-Mae, and for many years, a weekly phone call was slowly doing just that. Her death during my first season with the Festival had hit me harder than I ever thought it would have, and regret had become a permanent fixture on my conscience. And my heart.

"So, you think this case is going to be pretty cut and dried?" I asked.

"I'm hoping. If she did run away and if *her* family has an idea as to the crowd she was running with, the pieces of the past six years could come together quickly. Street life has a network all its own."

Jeffers' phone beeped. He popped the last of his waffle cone into his mouth and fished the device out of his pocket. His face fell as he read the text.

"But," he said, waggling the phone at me, "it seems things just got a lot more complicated."

Chapter 4

"He didn't say anything else?" Paul asked.

"You know he can't."

"I know he *shouldn't*. But that's never stopped him before."

"Before it was different," I said. "We were working together."

"You two were. I wasn't part of it, but I always knew more than I was supposed to."

Paul and I were out on his back deck. I had walked Moustache over when I'd finished with Jeffers and had just enough time for one of the portobello mushroom burgers Paul was grilling up before I had to head back to the theatre for my second show of the day. Moustache was underfoot trying to sous-chef while I lay in one of Paul's loungers feeling a little guilty for not helping.

The evening audience would see me as Louka in the George Bernard Shaw comedy, *Arms and the Man*.

The play is a love story with a heaping side dish of social commentary. The notions that war is pointless and people are hypocrites are presented in some of the wittiest writing ever to grace the stage.

The production had been such a triumph the season before that it was brought back by popular demand and continued to sell out. With the exception of me and one other actor, the cast was the same as the previous year. I'd inherited the part of the defiant and cunning housemaid trying to break down the barriers between the social classes from Manda Rogers, who was not with the Festival this year.

In the two seasons I had worked with Manda, there had been no love lost between us, and I was not sorry for her absence. I'd heard she'd become pregnant by the Russian director she had eloped with in the middle of the previous year and had been following him wherever his work took him. I'd also heard there was already trouble in paradise, which didn't surprise me given the impressive number of notches Manda had accumulated on her bedpost over the years.

One of the things I loved most about theatre was how the same roles could be played by hundreds of actors over time and yet never played the same way, each person bringing something of their distinct selves to the part. Every performance was as unique as a snowflake. And that's why plays had lives that extended far beyond their first inception. While it is true that I have the utmost respect for every actor who has ever played a role before me, I couldn't help but feel a small twinge of petty satisfaction whenever I heard someone say they preferred my Louka to Manda's.

"So, she'd been missing for approximately six years?" Paul asked.

"Yes."

"Her poor family. Having to lose her all over again now."

"Jeffers said there were counsellors available if we wanted to talk to someone about last night," I said, getting up and moving to the table.

"I'm okay. What about you?"

He slid a giant mushroom onto a bun and held it out to me. I added it to my plate along with a scoop of the Dijon potato and asparagus salad I had made earlier that morning.

"Counsellors aren't really my thing," I said.

"Nice of him to offer, though," he said, settling into the chair next to me.

Moustache dropped into a textbook perfect sit and waited to be rewarded for it with something from the table. I shook my head and pointed to his dish. His eyes followed my finger but returned immediately to my plate. I knew he'd give up eventually, but I also knew our dining would be underscored by subtle sighs and the odd whine.

"So, he didn't mention anything about—"

"Honey, I've told you everything Jeffers said. If there's anything more he can share, I'm sure he will. But for the moment—"

My phone rang. Jeffers' face popped up on the screen. I showed it to Paul and he quickly encouraged me to answer.

"Hi."

"Hi. Can you ask Paul if he knows a Gray Klassen?"

"You can ask him yourself. I'll put you on speaker."

The boys exchanged pleasantries and then Jeffers repeated his question.

"Jeez, that's a name I haven't heard in ages," Paul said.

"He would have been at high school with you."

"Yeah, I remember him. We weren't super close or anything. Nice enough guy, though."

"You don't happen to know where he's living now, do you?"

"Don't the police have ways of tracking people down?" I asked.

"We sure do," Jeffers said. "And this is one of them."

"Really? Nothing more advanced?"

"Like a board with flashing dots representing each and every person in a given area?"

"Yeah!"

"No."

Paul put us back on track. "I didn't keep in touch with him after we graduated. Like I said, we weren't close. I think I remember hearing his family moved to Fort Erie or something."

Fort Erie lies roughly forty minutes south of Niagara-on-the-Lake and is the last Canadian town before crossing the bridge over the Niagara River into Buffalo, New York.

"Yes. And from there he went to Toronto where he was recruited right out of university by CSIS and subsequently moved to Ottawa," Jeffers said.

"Ah, so there is some flashy thing," I said.

Jeffers chuckled but stuck to business. "He was working as a network analyst for a few years then got moved into field work. I was told he got an opportunity to relocate somewhere overseas and jumped at the chance, but I wasn't told where. The details are classified. That's as far as I got. I was hoping he might still be in touch with some old friends. His parents have both passed on."

"CSIS, wow," I said. "You might never find him."

The Canadian Security Intelligence Service is the country's lead agency in matters of national security—like the CIA and MI5 but lacking the black suits and sunglasses, and posh accents.

"CSIS employees are still allowed to have friends and families even if they do have to be discreet. Someone has to know something about him," Jeffers said.

"I can certainly ask around," Paul offered.

"What's this about?" I asked.

There was an intake of breath followed by silence. Jeffers was hesitating.

At that moment, a flash of gold streaked by us with a yowl and vanished through the pet flap in Paul's back door. Brimstone was a massive Maine Coon that Paul fed and housed and, in his own way, loved. It had been his fiancée's cat. After two previous attempts, Laura had committed suicide five years ago and her cat had crossed over to the dark side when she died. Paul saw snippets of the cuddly cat Brimstone had once been, but I saw only evil. A meaner cat did not exist.

Moustache let out a faint whimper, retreated under the table, and leaned hard against my legs. I knew whatever security the table or I could provide would be fleeting should Brimstone choose to unfurl his wrath, so I kept a close eye on the cat door lest extraordinary measures and superhuman manoeuvres became necessary.

Jeffers started speaking, oblivious to the drama playing out on the deck. "Gray's sister went missing a while back. Bernadelle Klassen."

"I remember that case," Paul said. "Klassen is such a common name. I didn't know she was Gray's sister. That's got to be ten years ago. At least."

"That's right," Jeffers said.

"Did they ever find her?" I asked.

"About five years after she went missing," Jeffers said.

Paul made a face that indicated the case hadn't had a positive outcome.

"She died in a similar way to our vic last night," Jeffers continued.

"What are you saying?" I asked. "You think there's a connection?"

Another hesitation. "We're exploring the possibility."

"Like a serial killer?"

'No, but—"

"Are there other women or just the two?"

"There's nothing—"

"But you just said—"

"Jeez, Samuel, it's too soon to know anything for sure. Right now, we're just looking to have a few conversations. Nothing to get too excited about."

"I'm not excited," I said.

Paul rolled his eyes. He knew my protestation was surface deep. In spite of the fact that I'd used up a couple of my nine lives helping Jeffers in the past, I'd do it again without hesitation.

"I'll see what I can find out about Gray," Paul said, effectively cutting off any further conversation that might have led to my offering, or Jeffers asking for, my assistance.

"Thanks," Jeffers said. "There's no rush but..."

"I'll get on it."

After Jeffers hung up, Paul looked at me. I took a bite of my burger, the picture of innocence.

"Bella?"

"What?"

"I see the wheels turning."

"There's no turning. There aren't even any wheels. I'm simply enjoying a nice—"

Moustache darted out from under the table, running for his life as Brimstone hissed and gave chase. We'd all been distracted by the possibility of multiple murders that we'd let our guards down. That was what the evil spawn had been waiting for. And now all hell was breaking loose.

"What happened to you?" Sean Maffey asked when I arrived at the theatre.

Sean was the stage manager for *Arms and the Man* and the clumsiest human being I had ever known.

The chase between cat and dog had resulted in drinking glasses being knocked over and flowerpots being upended. Dirt, dust, and fur flew while Paul and I climbed over and under patio furniture and through bushes to rescue Moustache from the feral feline fiend. A particularly dramatic dive roll had secured Moustache in Paul's arms and a moment's distraction from me had enabled us to reach the safety of the house. We then watched from behind the sliding door as Brimstone walked through the melee, surveying his destruction with satisfaction, before flicking his tail at us and wandering off to wherever his portal to hell was located.

My shirt sported a mix of dirt, grass stains, and Paul's Diet Coke, and my leg boasted a bloody scratch where Brimstone had caught me. Paul had aggravated an old shoulder injury during his gymnastics routine, and Moustache had lost tufts of fur and much of his dignity. Only Brimstone had walked away from the ordeal unscathed.

"I could ask you the same thing," I said to Sean, who was wearing a shirt with a similar design to mine.

"Oh," he said, sheepishly. "I had a run-in with the lion, the witch, and the wardrobe this afternoon during Narnia.

Haven't had a chance to change." He laughed and waved it off.

In the months I'd worked with Sean, I'd never seen him despair over his clumsiness. He always maintained a sense of humour, even at the height of awkwardness. It was something I found incredibly endearing about him.

"Fortunately for me, I have a costume to escape into," I said with a sympathetic smile and continued on my way to the dressing room.

A small group of people were huddled around a computer in the green room when I walked by.

"What's going on?" I asked.

"Press conference. It just ended," Jarod Riley said and fell into step with me. "You're a mess. Big fight with the boyfriend?"

I laughed and shook my head.

Jarod had spent much of my first year at the Shaw trying to get me to go out with him. We ran in different shows the year after, which kept me off his radar, but fate had reunited us this season, and he was, unapologetically, back at it.

"What was the press conference?" I asked.

"The woman from the drive-in. Her family was making a statement."

"Really?" It was odd that Jeffers hadn't mentioned it. He said they'd ID'd her but nothing about going public so soon. "What did they say?"

"The usual: they're heartbroken; they won't rest until they find the person who did this. That kind of thing. The whole thing is horrible. I can't imagine what they're going through. And then to have cameras shoved in their faces and be forced to have to—"

"If they agreed to a press conference presumably—"

"Well, it was more like coverage of the family arriving at the police station."

"You said it was a press conference."

"Well … it…" We arrived at my dressing room. "Listen, I'm sure there's going to be more on tonight's news. Do you want to get a drink after the show? We can watch it together."

I politely declined, although I knew it most certainly would be the late-night lead story and I definitely would need a drink when I watched it.

Chapter 5

Paul had the television on and the drinks poured when I arrived with three minutes to spare before the news started. Jarod had accepted my refusal as he had all my others, with misguided hope and optimism. Moustache didn't greet me when I came in. He just looked up at me from his bed on the floor with a woebegone sigh and waited for me to come to him. I smothered him with kisses and he gave a half-hearted wag of his tail.

"He's still sulking?" I asked.

"Yep. We both are," Paul said, readjusting the heating pad he had on his shoulder.

"Do you need kisses, too?"

"Maybe," he said.

I joined him on the couch and laid a gentle kiss on his shoulder. "Better?"

He shook his head and tapped a finger on his cheek.

I kissed where the finger had directed me. "How's that?"

He gave my question a moment's contemplation before shaking his head again and sticking out his lower lip. This time his finger tapped his mouth.

"Poor sweet baby," I cooed. "Did the mean cat hurt your wittle wips?"

He laughed in spite of himself but quickly restored his pout. I brought my face to his and kissed him lightly while theme music announced the beginning of the broadcast. And an actual, bona fide, press conference.

Jeffers was at a podium flanked by a number of people I didn't recognize. There were a man and woman in uniform and a woman in a business suit whom I took to be there in some kind of official capacity. There were also two couples—a man and woman in their fifties, I guessed, and a twenty-something woman holding the hand of a man who looked slightly older. Both women were weeping.

"On the evening of Friday, July 6," Jeffers began, "officers from the Niagara Regional Police were called to the Can-View Drive-In in Fonthill in response to the discovery of human remains. Upon arrival, we found the body of a female in a dumpster. Following an autopsy by the office of the chief medical examiner, the victim has been identified as twenty-one-year-old Milla Ward, and the death has been deemed suspicious. We do not believe Ms. Ward's death was the result of a random attack and investigators are working around the clock to bring those responsible to justice. We encourage anyone who may have information about this incident to contact the NRP. I will now take questions."

Jeffers informed disappointed reporters that no further details about the cause or circumstances of Milla's death would be disclosed at present but did reveal that police were not actively searching for any kind of weapon. He also went on to field questions about the review of CCTV footage and possible witnesses but refused to answer any questions about Milla's background or speculate on events that may have led to her death. I noticed he skirted a question about whether her death was believed to be an isolated incident.

The final question was about the drive-in itself.

"It is believed that Ms. Ward's body was brought to the venue after she had been killed. The drive-in is open for business as usual and is considered absolutely safe. At this time, I would like to invite the victim's uncle to make a statement on behalf of the family."

The man who'd been standing off to the left took over Jeffers' place at the podium. The script at the bottom of the screen identified him as Milla's uncle, Rodney Koepper.

"Our family is in complete shock over the death of our Milla," he said, reading a prepared statement. "We would like to express our deepest thanks to the NRP for the empathy and compassion we've received during this difficult time. We are in full support of the police as they continue to investigate in the hopes of finding answers, and we beg anyone with information to come forward. But our hearts are broken, so we would like to have the chance to mourn privately. Thank you."

Jeffers offered his final thanks and ushered everyone away from the podium amid hurled questions and flashing cameras.

"He still didn't say anything about the baby," Paul said, muting the TV.

"No," I said. "Nor about a possible link to other cases."

"Probably hoping to weed out false confessions."

"Look at you being all policey." I said.

"I've watched my share of cop dramas," Paul said proudly.

"Oh yeah, Columbo? What else?"

"Credibility. If someone knows details that have been withheld, they're a credible witness."

"I'm impressed."

"Yeah?"

"Yeah. I'm even a little turned on."

"Really?" he said, turning off his heating pad and tossing it to the floor. He slid one arm around my waist. "Well, let me show you what else I've learned from the TV."

My phone sounded an outrageously early ping the following morning. I had forgotten to set it to Do Not Disturb.

Paul was asleep beside me, oblivious. I rolled over, ignoring the text notification, but was called back by another. Against my better judgment, I reached for my phone. The texts were from Jeffers.

Samuel?

You awake?

I typed my response: *No.*

A ping. *Oh good. I'm coming over.*

Jeffers, no, I typed. *It's*—I fumbled to check the time—*not even 7 a.m.!*

I've got cinnamon buns.

Later!

Cream cheese icing...

No!

Aria made them.

Aria Jeffers was an amazing cook. Many of our work sessions in the past had been catered by Aria, even when she was in the late stages of pregnancy and the early stages of nursing. Now, with a toddler underfoot, she had added baking to her repertoire. She had a superhero cape in her closet, I was sure.

I didn't know whether she was complicit in her husband's bribery and manipulation through food, but my stomach grumbled and I decided I didn't care.

I'm at Paul's.

I decided to let Paul sleep and was in the process of making the world's quietest pot of coffee when Jeffers arrived. The scent of cinnamon filled the air and my mouth starting watering. Moments later Moustache appeared in the kitchen.

We took our breakfast to the back deck so we could talk rather than whisper. After all his attempts at sampling Aria's masterpiece were thwarted, Moustache became engrossed in carefully examining the aftermath of the previous day's battle and scuttled around the yard with his nose to the ground.

"Give me one of those rolls," I said. "They're the only reason I let you come."

Jeffers laughed and slid a plump, perfectly iced, cinnamon spiral onto a plate. While I was basking in its glory, Jeffers dropped three file folders onto the table.

"What are these?" I asked, reaching out to open the one nearest me.

"Don't get your sticky fingers all over them."

My hands happily went back to the cinnamon goodness and let Jeffers do the honours.

"Milla Ward, Bernadelle Klassen, Angela Hansen."

As he said each name, Jeffers opened the folders to reveal photographs of the women.

"So, there *is* a serial killer," I said, sitting up straight and licking cream cheese icing off my fingers.

"Still too soon for that, but we believe there is a connection."

He picked up the folder containing the details of Bernadelle Klassen's final moments.

"Bernadelle's body was found five years ago," Jeffers said. "She'd been missing for five years prior to that. She was last seen leaving a grocery store in Fort Erie where she worked. She'd finished her shift at nine that evening and was walking home like she always did. At the time, none of her family, friends, or co-workers mentioned anything odd about her behaviour on that day or the days leading up to her disappearance. She and her boyfriend of nine years had broken up three months earlier, but according to everyone the police spoke to, she was a happy twenty-three-year-old."

"Nine years? And she was only twenty-three?"

"They met when they were fourteen. Stayed together when he went away to university in Alberta. He got a job out there shortly after he graduated and asked her to join him but she wanted to stay here. Close to her folks."

I studied the pictures of Bernadelle. She did look happy. In one of the most recent pictures taken, however, I thought I saw a tightness around her mouth when she smiled. Like she was trying to prove to whoever was taking the picture just how happy she was. The last few photos in the file were of her body.

"She was found in the Niagara Gorge," Jeffers said. "Someone went to great pains to make it look like an accident. Like she'd fallen and hit her head and drowned. Forensics show she died of a pulmonary embolism due to a blood clot. The blow to the head and putting her in the water were just for show."

The Niagara Gorge begins at the base of Niagara Falls and runs through to the escarpment in Queenston, a neighbouring village of Niagara-on-the-Lake. With daredevils barrelling over the Falls and thrill-seekers riding the rapids in kayaks, the gorge has swallowed many a life. But with legitimate hiking accidents also leading to death, it wasn't an unreasonable way to try to dispose of a body.

"Any idea where she was for five years?" I asked.

Jeffers shook his head and opened Angela Hansen's file.

"Angela Hansen, thirty-one, was missing for three years before her body was found. That was two years ago. She suffered from bipolar disorder and, at the time of her disappearance, had been in the throes of a manic episode. She was also five months pregnant. Her husband said she'd gone off her meds out of concern for the baby. She worked at the local radio station. Had a morning show that was really popular. Evidently, on the day in question, she was spouting nonsense on air. Listeners were calling in, expressing their concern. Her colleagues couldn't get her out of the booth. The police were called and eventually her husband arrived and convinced her to go home. He said he gave her a sedative, put her to bed, and went back to work. When he got home a few hours later, she was gone."

"Does the husband check out?"

"Yeah."

"And how did she die?"

Jeffers flipped over a photograph. My stomach turned at the sight of the woman's badly decomposed body.

"Multiple organ failure due to septic shock from an infection. She was found in an orchard by some seasonal workers. The medical examiner figured her body had been there for several weeks and had been badly treated by the elements."

Moustache returned from surveying the combat zone and ran to Jeffers, putting his paws on his thigh and rising up on his hind legs for a scratch. His back end wiggled, indicating his dignity had recovered overnight. Jeffers stroked the dog's ears and Moustache leaned into the massage.

Jeffers closed Angela Hansen's file. He didn't open Milla Ward's. Neither of us needed a reminder as to how she died.

"It turns out Milla Ward had a blockage in her colon. It forced her womb out of shape and cut down on the oxygen supply for the baby, which resulted in brain damage and the other deformities. It's a miracle he survived at all, let alone for as long as he did."

"More than a miracle," I said.

Jeffers nodded then added, "It's believed Milla had already lost a lot of blood due to a hemorrhage before the C-section was done and then kept on bleeding during and after the procedure. The official cause of death was blood loss."

"They're all seemingly natural causes of death," I said.

"Yes, but treatable if caught in time. It's possible these women were allowed to die, and that makes their deaths manslaughter at the very least. The fact that the women had been missing and the bodies were moved after death only adds to the suspicion. We ran a tox screen on Milla just in case something else might have been at play, but the lab is getting a much-needed upgrade so all the tests are being sent out. Will be a while before we get the results."

"Have you found out anything about the circumstances leading up to her disappearance?" I asked.

"She left home at fifteen. She and her sister had been living with their aunt and uncle. Their parents had both been in and out of the system and officially lost custody of the girls when Milla was seven and her sister was eleven. They'd been placed in foster care for a time and eventually their father's brother and his wife took them in. According to Sarah, the sister, Milla and her uncle fought a lot and Milla couldn't wait to get out of the house. She finally left one evening after a particularly big row and no one in the family has heard from her since."

"Okay, but I'm not sure I understand," I said. "You think these deaths are connected, but they all died in different ways, their ages when they went missing are all over the place, their backgrounds are completely different, and there's nothing even physically similar to suggest 'a type'..."

"But they do have something in common."

"I don't see it."

"All of their deaths were childbirth related."

"What?"

"Bernadelle Klassen had given birth four weeks before she died. Angela Hansen died within days of delivery. And Milla Ward died during her C-section. And that's not everything. All three women had had multiple births."

"So..."

Jeffers spoke slowly. "We think Milla Ward and the others may have been surrogates for a baby-selling ring."

"Are you serious?"

Jeffers nodded. "And there are probably others. All it takes is one medical complication to add them to this list. We're running the records of missing women who have turned up dead as well as those who fit the profile and might still be working for these guys."

"You think these women are doing this willingly?"

"I don't know."

"Is that why you didn't mention the baby last night at the press conference?"

He nodded again. "Special Investigative Services have been looking into a possible organization for some time."

"Oh my god."

"Look, I want to be clear. We don't know for certain that such an organization even exists or that our three vics were involved. It could all be a dead end. Or it just might lead us to their killers."

"I understand," I said. "But why are you telling me this?"

Jeffers hesitated then said, "Inspector Morris asked me to bring you in for a meeting."

I had met Roger Morris several times and had been on the receiving end of both his reproaches and his praise. He was in no way a physically imposing man. He was slight in stature, gentle in manners, and mild of voice. But any doubts about his power vanished after a moment or two in his presence. As much as I'd loved working with Jeffers in the past, a run-in with Morris was never something I looked forward to.

"Why?" I asked. My stomach had begun doing backflips at the mere thought. "Morris has made exceptions for my involvement in the past but he was always very clear that he did not like it."

"Eat your bun. You'll feel better with something in your stomach," Jeffers said, sensing my nerves.

I did as I was told although I barely registered the taste.

"I didn't ask questions. If Morris thinks you can help, then you can help."

"How?" I asked, my mouth full.

"He wants you to buy a baby."

Chapter 6

"You're not really going to buy one," Morris explained, "but we want you to go through the process as if you are."

Morris' office was so large he looked small in it. He sat behind a sturdy oak desk facing Jeffers and me. We were joined by Staff Sergeant Lester Crayne, who was the head of the Special Investigative Services Section and Constable Lindsey Ambegaokar, who was part of the Drugs and Morality Unit team.

"Call me Lindsey," she said when I stumbled over her last name. "Everyone does. Ambegaokar's a mouthful."

She sat in a chair identical to the ones Jeffers and I were sitting in while Crayne stood to the right of Morris' desk. Other than their names and departments, I hadn't been told anything else about them.

"Um," I began but was silenced by the slight raise of Morris' index finger.

He motioned to Crayne, who took up the conch. "Ms. James, what we do in SIS is collect information about organized criminal activity that we pass along to the appropriate units within the police force, who then take whatever action is required. Sometimes immediately, sometimes over a substantial period of time."

I guessed Crayne was in his mid to late fifties. His hair was mostly blond except for a shock of grey hair over his left ear, and the lines around his mouth and eyes gave evidence of a life full of laughter. I was comforted by the fact that, despite the nature of his work, he was a man who found things to smile about. He spoke to me respectfully without a whiff of condescension or impatience. Like I was one of the team. I liked him instantly.

"One of our units is Drugs and Morality," he said. "It's divided into three smaller sections and Lindsey here is one of the members of the Morality team. They investigate drug trafficking, prostitution, illegal gambling, and other morality offences."

"Like selling babies on the black market," I said.

"Yes. I'll let Lindsey fill you in on the details, but, basically, we've been tracking some individuals over the past several years who we believe are involved in the illegal sale of newborns. We've been monitoring these people, and the recent death of Milla Ward has given us what we need to finally take action. And that's what we're hoping you'll help us with."

"Why me?" I asked.

"These people and organizations pride themselves on invisibility," Lindsey said.

She was older than me but just slightly. Her hair was swept back into a perfect messy bun, and she wore a sleeveless blouse that showed off enviably toned arms. She was more than comfortable in the company of men more powerful than she was and knew when to hold back, as she had when both Morris and Crayne spoke, but she also knew how to take command of a room, as she did now.

"All transactions are off the books. It's called a shadow economy. Nothing is reported or recorded. There are no traces left of any kind. There is no red tape to get through, no application process, no judgment of lifestyle choices or religious beliefs. Essentially, if you have the money and know where to go, you can buy whatever you want, no questions asked. And no one will ever know. In theory, anyway."

"I understand all that," I said. "What I don't understand is my place in it. I mean, you must have people trained to work undercover. You don't need an actress."

"No, we don't," Morris said. "We need a celebrity."

"I don't follow."

"Well, first off, with any luck, they'd recognize you so they'd know you're not a cop," Crayne said.

"Also, and I want to be clear," Lindsey said, "we're not saying celebrities are regular consumers of black-market items. But there are reasons why a black-market adoption might be attractive to someone in the public eye."

"Such as?"

"Often the details of a famous person's lifestyle are widely known—history of addiction, sexual partners, arrests or trouble with the law, political and religious affiliations. You get the idea. There's not a lot that celebrities can keep hidden. That's what sells magazines."

"And all of those things could hinder a traditional, mainstream adoption?"

"Yes. There are also less provocative reasons why a celebrity might look for alternative means. It's not uncommon to want to hide fertility struggles and, unfortunately, looking to parent without a partner or to parent with a same-sex partner are still big issues for some adoption agencies. And did you know it's nearly impossible to qualify for a mainstream adoption if you've ever suffered from a mental illness?"

That alone would disqualify half of the world's celebrities, I was sure.

"On top of all that, there have been cases of adoption agencies selling information. Suddenly, photographers are hiding in the bushes when a celebrity shows up for an appointment. And then there's timing. A legal adoption process is lengthy, and there have been instances of mothers reneging on the adoption agreement once babies are born. None of that is an issue with illegal adoptions. People can get what they want, when they want it, with no risk of disappointment."

"Many celebrities strive for privacy whenever they can get it," Crayne said. "Often they're willing to pay for it, whatever it may be and whatever the price."

"And then what? They spin some story about adopting an orphan from war-torn here or drought-stricken there so the same tabloids that have tarnished their chances at a legal adoption and forced them to pursue extreme measures all of a sudden praise their nobility and nominate them for Parent of the Year?" All eyes stared at me in surprise. "I'm sorry. I didn't mean for that to come out sounding so cynical. And I'm certainly not blaming people for going this route, especially if they have no other choice. In my mind, if someone is willing to go to such extremes to become a parent, you know those babies are going to be loved and given the best lives possible. But I'm having a hard time wrapping my head around this. Around the fact that something like this even exists. I mean, I know there's an underbelly. I know that. But there is also a price that is a whole lot more than whatever people are paying for these babies."

"Get Ms. James a glass of water," Morris said to Jeffers.

"I'm fine. But thank you."

"Ms. James, what's troubling you is the same thing that's troubling us. It has little to do with the people who turn to this particular alternative and everything to do with how those babies are coming into the world and what is happening to their mothers. Believe me when I tell you, we are all angry."

I met Morris' eyes. He might have tolerated my involvement with Jeffers in the past, but this time he was appealing to me for help. He was not a man one said no to. Nor would one wish to.

"I don't have that kind of money."

"We'll take care of all that," Crayne said.

'I'm not even sure I have that kind of celebrity."

"Ms. James," Morris said, "you may not have paparazzi following your every move, but you do have a national fan base and a strong one at that. In addition, you have a history, a very public history, of keeping your private life out of the papers. In my research, you have been something of a thorn in the sides of tabloid journalists."

I smiled at the charge. It was true. I had carefully managed my rise to fame, such as it was, during *Port Authority* and beyond. I understood the give and take of public relations and always gave enough to fulfill my end but no more. And even that was never really enough to hold a reader's attention. The juiciest bits the media ever got were about my relationship with my *Port Authority* co-star, Rich Arborall, which really didn't bother me, since our five-year relationship was more of a publicity stunt than anything else. We had genuinely liked one another, but our coming together turned out to be better for the show than it was for either of us, and we had stayed together longer than we ever should have because of that.

I'd spent years restricting access—mastering the art of when to step into the spotlight and knowing exactly how long to stay and how much to reveal.

"That's what makes you ideal," Crayne said. "You have an established history as an extremely private person. It would make complete sense that you would choose an alternative to traditional adoption."

"But why would I?" I asked. "I have nothing shady in my background. I've got absolutely nothing to hide. On paper, I'm an ideal prospective parent."

"I think what Staff Sergeant Crayne is saying, Ms. James, is that it would make complete sense to *them*," Morris clarified. "To the individuals running the organization. Besides, most people with nothing to hide always have at least one skeleton in the closet. The people running this organization know that and that's what they count on."

"They also want invisibility because they don't want any attention drawn to their illegal operation," Crayne said. "They're going to assume that your demand for privacy stems from you trying to keep hidden whatever your skeleton might be."

"And, ultimately, they're not going to care one way or the other so long as they get their money," Lindsey put in.

I exhaled loudly. "I don't know where I'd even begin," I said. "I don't—"

"That's why I'm here," Jeffers said, speaking for the first time since we'd arrived.

"Detective Sergeant Jeffers has been working with Staff Sergeant Crayne and Constable Ambegaokar and their team," Morris said, "He'll be doing most of the work. And he'll be with you every step of the way."

I looked over to Jeffers and he gave me a wink.

"If you agree, Ms. James, we can start working out the details. There are quite a few, I'm sure you can imagine," Morris said.

"Partners again, Samuel?" Jeffers said. "What do you say?"

Chapter 7

"Absolutely not!" Paul said.

He'd been pacing the length of my living room ever since Jeffers introduced the idea of my helping with the case. Moustache was perched on his armchair following Paul's movements with his head.

"I'm sorry. I shouldn't have said that," he said to me. "You know I'm not 'that guy.' I'd never say you couldn't do something. But you can't be serious. Look what's happened before!"

"It'll be different this time," I said.

"You said that last time. And you ended up nearly being strangled in a boiler room."

"I know but—"

"And the time before that you were buried alive."

"That was just because—"

"Just because what, Bells, what?"

I didn't know how to answer. He was right about everything he'd said. I'd used up two of my lives in my past involvement with Jeffers and wasn't sure if I could count on having another seven to see me through.

Paul stopped pacing and leaned against one of the walls forming the archway that led from the hallway into the living room. Jeffers sat on one side of the sofa with the ankle of one leg resting on the thigh of the other, his elbow propped up on an armrest holding his chin. I sat on the other side, hunched over, my forearms on my knees and my hands clenched. With nothing happening, Moustache dangled his front paws over the edge of the chair and rested his head on top of them with sigh. In the silence that followed, the faces of Milla Ward, Bernadelle Klassen, and Angela Hansen looked up at us from their folders on the coffee table.

Jeffers had laid out the details for Paul as he had done with me that morning. I had insisted we tell Paul as much as we could. We didn't need his permission, but we wanted his support. And I didn't want any secrets between us.

Paul's eyes were locked on the photos, and whatever passed between him and the women in that moment seemed to soften his resolve. "Where's my bribe?" he asked.

"What?" I asked.

"My bribe. Aria always makes something for you when Jeffers wants you to do something, so where's mine?"

"In the car," Jeffers said.

Paul and I both shot Jeffers an equally surprised look.

"Really?" I asked.

Jeffers nodded. "Seafood linguine."

"What kind of sauce?" Paul asked.

"Alfredo."

Paul's shoulders slumped. He made it a habit to eat healthy, but he was powerless against a good Alfredo.

"Tiger shrimp, crab, scallops," Jeffers said. "The big ones—not those baby ones."

"He gets tiger shrimp and I get cinnamon rolls?" I said.

"I knew I needed to pull out the big guns," Jeffers said.

Paul was still leaning against the wall, his arms crossed. He was steeling himself against what we all knew was inevitable.

"Oh, and there are butter tarts too," Jeffers said.

What remained of Paul's determination crumbled. "I will share the linguine, but the butter tarts are mine," he said, walking into the kitchen.

"Are you sure you want to do this?" Paul asked me later that night while we both stared at the ceiling.

Our reasons for being awake were completely different.

I knew Paul was worried. He'd been quiet through dinner and had excused himself shortly afterward to get ahead on some paperwork, taking the butter tarts with him. When I looked in on him after Jeffers left, his attempt to minimize the window on his computer screen was a split second too slow, and I saw that he'd been researching the dangers of black-market dealings.

I, on the other hand, was awake because I was being punished for overindulging in Aria's linguine.

"I have to," I said.

"You don't," he said, rolling over to face me. "You have no obligation to Morris. You're not a cop. You don't have to do anything. Just tell him—"

"It's not Morris," I said. "It's Milla. You saw what they did to her. To her baby."

"Yes, I did but—"

"And Angela, and Bernadelle, and who knows how many other women."

"And you? What if you end up on that list?"

We stared at each other in the darkness. I reached out to caress his face.

"These guys…" Paul said. "The people who run these kinds of things … they're dangerous, Bells."

"I know," I said. "Which is why the police will have my back. It's different this time."

"I think it's really great you want to help," he said, taking my hand and bringing it to his lips. "It's one of the things I love most about you but——"

"What are some of the other things?" I said.

"What?"

"You said it's *one* of the things you love about me," I said, sliding my hand under the covers. "I bet I can guess something else you love." I brought my lips to his to end the conversation.

I knew we could talk about it until we were both blue in the face, but nothing was going to change. I was going to help Jeffers, and Paul was going to worry. I thought it best to shift the focus to something we could both agree on.

"You look happy," Jeffers said, as I climbed the steps to the NRP's front entrance where Jeffers was holding the door open for me. "I was worried you and Paul might throw down after I left last night."

I laughed. "No, we're all good."

Jeffers expedited my way through security and led me down hallways and upstairs to where his desk sat in the open-concept office he shared with the five other Detective Sergeants and one Detective Constable who made up the Homicide division of the Major Crimes Unit.

Jeffers' desk was in the corner and, the way the partitions and built-in cabinetry wrapped themselves around it, allowed for as much privacy as one could hope for in a shared space.

Lindsey had pulled a chair over to Jeffers' area and was awaiting our arrival while a young man sat in Jeffers' seat, typing away madly on a keyboard. Both his and Lindsey's eyes were fixed on the two monitors that occupied Jeffers' desktop.

"Okay, are we all set?" Jeffers asked.

Lindsey looked up, smiled when she saw me, and stood to offer me her chair.

"I'm just inputting a few final details," the young man at the controls said.

"This is Steven Mears," Lindsey said. "He's one of our technical analysts."

Steven shot a "hello" over his shoulder and continued typing. Jeffers leaned over his shoulder to watch.

"Can I get you anything? Coffee?" Lindsey asked.

"No, thank you," I said. "It wouldn't sit well. I'm a little nervous, to be honest."

"Nothing to be nervous about," she said, giving me a smile.

"Okay, I think we're good to go," Steven said. "I had to clear up some space on your computer so I could download the Tor browser. I also set up a new VPN—we obviously can't use the department's—and we don't want anyone tracing your IP back to here."

"What if someone asks why I'm using a VPN?"

"No one will. Everyone down there uses them. Nobody wants to be tracked by the cops."

Jeffers and Lindsey nodded while I put on my best "I totally get you" face even though all of what Steven said had sailed swiftly over my head. TOR, VPN, IP—the letters bounced off each other inside my brain, adding to my confusion.

"I've set up your Bitcoin Wallet and Dream Market accounts. Your handles and passwords for both are here," he said, indicating a lime-green post-it stuck to the side of one of the monitors. "I've also set up notifications to come to a phone that we'll monitor in Siberia."

"Siberia?" I asked.

"It's where all the computer servers are and where we techies spend most of our time. Kind of like mission control. I don't know why it's called Siberia. You can imagine the amount of heat these things give off."

"Maybe they were alluding to more of the exile-type reputation—"

"Anyway," he said, turning his attention back to Jeffers before I could finish, "these are the handles we've flagged as possible kingpins." He pointed to a purple post-it next to the lime-green one. "These are the guys you want to deal with. If anyone different gets in touch with you, we'll screen them and let you know whether to engage or brush them off."

"Copy," Jeffers said.

"And here," Steven said, clicking on a file folder on Jeffers' computer screen, "is how you start the TOR browser. From there it's just a couple of clicks and you're into Dream Market."

"I'm sorry," I said, unable to keep up the charade. "I have no idea what you're talking about."

"We're talking about the dark web, Samuel," Jeffers said.

"The what?"

"The dark web," Steven said. "The internet available to the public through common browsers like Chrome or

Firefox is only about four percent of what exists. Most information is hidden and only accessible if you have a special search engine like Tor. Once you're in, you can browse and talk anonymously."

"And buy and sell things that are illegal through websites like Dream Market," Lindsey added.

"Drugs, weapons, hit man services, pornography…"

"It all relies on heavy encryption," Lindsey said. "Even the transactions are done via cryptocurrencies, like Bitcoin."

"That's why it's so important to have a good VPN," Steven said.

I shook my head.

"A virtual private network?"

"Sorry."

"All computers can be identified by their IP address. You've heard of that, right?"

I nodded.

"Right. So, anyone can find out what sites you've been visiting and even where your computer is located through your IP if they want to. A VPN basically hides that address to make it look like your computer is physically located somewhere else."

"It makes people virtually untraceable," Lindsey said.

"If everyone using the dark web has one of these, how are we supposed to find these guys?" I asked.

"She said 'virtually,'" Jeffers said with a wink. "That's why we pay Steve-O here the big bucks."

"Yeah, right. Okay, you should have enough to get started," Steven said. "Let me know if you run into any trouble."

When Steven left, Jeffers took up his position in front of the computer. I slid my chair next to him and Lindsey perched on the edge of a filing cabinet.

"Surely you don't need me for this part. If all this is anonymous, what does my celebrity even matter? What difference will it make? It sounds to me like these guys, whoever they are, don't care who they're selling to as long as the sale goes through."

"That's exactly right," Lindsey said. "If it is a ring, like we suspect, there's no telling how big it is or how far it reaches. This is just one of the avenues we're exploring. And only one of many ways these people could be doing business."

"I don't follow."

"We also think they have other, legitimate businesses through which they can facilitate this kind of activity. And infiltrating those is going to require a personal connection. Also, there is the chance, albeit minute, that one of these people may want to meet. Not actually face-to-face, but something that allows them to observe you. These guys can smell cops a mile away. All these businesses could possibly be in collusion," she said, gesturing to a stack of file folders held together by a rainbow of rubber bands. "We've sent undercover teams in before, and none of them have been able to make even an inch of headway. I don't know what it is we cops give off, but they sniff us out every time."

"So, it's because of how I smell?"

"Trust me, Samuel," Jeffers said. "If we thought we could do this without you, you'd be home with your feet up."

"Well, we better get started then," I said.

We all watched intently as Jeffers launched the browser and logged on to the Dream Market website.

The site looked like any of the marketplace sites I'd visited, but instead of browsing for antiques or furniture, the categories were much like what Steven had described. Every possible drug you could imagine, weaponry I'd never heard of, and things of a sexual nature that left me feeling like I needed a bath. The list of what was available went on and on. You really could get whatever your wildest dreams thought up. The market was aptly named.

Jeffers scrolled until he found a category to suit our purpose and clicked the appropriate geographical filters.

I shuddered.

Jeffers looked over at me and gave me a reassuring smile. "You ready?"

I nodded.

He typed, *Looking for a newborn.*

Lindsey gave a nod and he hit Enter.

"Now what?" I asked.

"Now we wait."

"And in the meantime," Lindsey said, "we can start going through these." She indicated the file folders again.

The phone on Jeffers' desk rang. He listened intently to the voice on the other end then responded with "Tell him I'll be right out." He hung up the receiver and turned to me. "There's someone I want you to meet. Lindsey, we'll take these with us, if that's okay?" She nodded. "We'll go through them today and I'll fill Bella in what you and I have already discussed."

"Sounds good," she said. "Call me if you have any questions."

"You feel like a hot dog?" Jeffers asked me when Lindsey had gone.

"It's not even eleven."

"So?"

"I thought we had to meet someone."

"Meet and eat, Samuel. Trick of the trade. Food takes some of the formality out of things and the more relaxed people feel, the more they have to say. And, besides, the hot dog guy sells out fast during the lunch hour. Best to get there early."

"Does he have sausages?"

"Bratwurst, knockwurst. It's a wurst lover's paradise."

Chapter 8

"Mr. Koepper, it's nice to see you," Jeffers said, offering his hand to the man I immediately recognized from the press conference.

He had a neatly trimmed beard and moustache that were both greyer than his sandy brown hair. At the time I had placed him in his fifties but seeing him in person told me I'd overshot it. The facial hair aged him slightly, but he couldn't have been more than forty-five. He wore a crisp, short-sleeved madras shirt buttoned to the collar and equally crisp chinos. The whole look, from the part in his hair to his polished loafers, projected a squeaky-clean image. If he'd had a tie and a cardigan, he'd surely have given Mr. Rogers a run for his money.

"Detective Jeffers, I'm sorry to barge in on you like this," Rodney Koepper said, shaking Jeffers' hand. "But I was hoping you might have a few minutes?"

"Of course. Rodney, I told you my door is always open. Bella and I were just heading over to the hot dog cart. Why don't you join us?"

Koepper hesitated and looked at me.

"Forgive me. I forgot you two haven't been introduced. Bella, this is Rodney Koepper. He's Milla Ward's uncle, as you know. Rodney, this is Bella. She just joined the team investigating your niece's death."

Technically, everything Jeffers had said was true, but how he'd said it and the omission of my somewhat-famous surname made it sound like I held a much more official position in the department than I actually did.

"It's very nice to meet you, Detective…?" Rodney said, extending his hand to me.

"Bella's fine," I said with as sympathetic and welcoming a smile as I could muster. I'd worked with Jeffers long enough to know when I was supposed to play along.

Rodney's eyes met mine as we shook hands. His grip was warm and gentle. He broke the clasp quickly but his eyes stayed on mine. It was like he could see into my soul. Like the glasses he wore gave him some kind of x-ray vision. I didn't know how much his superpower could tell him about me, but I lowered my gaze and almost tripped as I made a hasty retreat down the steps and through the door Jeffers was holding. The bright sun was glorious and gave me just the excuse I needed to hide behind my sunglasses.

The farmer's market, which was across the street from the police station, had picnic tables scattered around its perimeter. On market days, the tables were busy with patrons who were keen to fill their bellies as well as their shopping bags. Hot offerings of perogies, empanadas, and falafel were among the many lunch options favoured by the locals. Paul absolutely loved the samosas. Today, the tables were occupied by fellow hot dog early birds and many office workers grabbing a quick cigarette and sipping coffee out of travel mugs.

It was another scorching day, so I was surprised by how many people were choosing to sit in the sun. We chose a table in the shade, out of the UV rays' harmful reach. And out of earshot.

Rodney seemed nervous in our company and picked at the toppings on his hot dog.

"I know you're busy," he said. "And I know you promised to keep us informed but I … I don't know what to do. I feel like I need to do something … for Milla but…"

"It's good you stopped by," Jeffers said and Rodney visibly relaxed. "There are a few things we'd like to talk to you about."

"Have there been some developments?" Rodney sounded full of hope. "Have you found the person who did this?"

"Rodney, we're doing everything we can," Jeffers said. "Right now, what we need is a bit more information, which we hope will give us a better idea of where Milla might have been and who she was with."

"I told you we haven't seen Milla since she left home. The phone call from the police was the first we'd heard about her in years."

"Can we talk a little more about why Milla left?" Jeffers asked.

Rodney sighed and put down the untouched hot dog. "I'm afraid that was my fault. I put too much pressure on her. I was overprotective. I wanted so badly to keep her from following in her parents' footsteps, I forgot she was just a little girl and that what she needed, more than anything, was a normal childhood. I drove her to the very life I was trying to keep her from."

"You were just trying to help," I said.

"Was I? Or was I just fuelled by fear and frustration?"

"How do you mean?"

"My brother, Jonas, Milla's dad, was a difficult child. A difficult everything, actually. He likely suffered from ADHD and some other behavioural disorders that were never diagnosed or treated because, back then, those things weren't. As a result, my mother cried, my father hit, and I cowered. Dad kicked Jonas out when he was way too young to be on his own, but life had become unbearable at home and there was really no other alternative." He paused. "Actually, that's not true. There are always alternatives, as I've come to learn, but it was a different time and..."

"Did things get better once Jonas was gone?" I asked.

"For us? Oh, yes. We slowly became a family again. But for Jonas, no. As you'd expect. What's out there for a teenage boy with nothing? He did whatever he could for money. Spent that money on drugs. And that was the cycle he fell into. He'd show up at the house from time to time when he knew Dad would be out and Mom would cry to see him and give him whatever food and money she could. Eventually, he stopped coming around. I'd see him on the street sometimes. He and Claudia, the girls' mother, used to panhandle outside the bus terminal. One day I saw she was pregnant and I told my parents. I don't know exactly what my father did, but I never saw them outside the bus station again.

"A few years later, they came by with their little Sarah. Claudia was pregnant again. They said they had a place to live and both had jobs and were off whatever they'd been on. They offered Dad some money. To pay him back, they said. He didn't take it. Things never healed completely, but we all tried. For several years, we all saw each other regularly. Mom was there when Claudia gave birth to Milla. She loved being a grandma to the girls. But then things started to change. We saw less and less of them, and when we did see them, it was clear they had fallen back on hard times. Eventually, they vanished from our lives completely. I spent a couple of years trying to find them and finally learned the girls had been put into the foster system and that Jonas was in jail and Claudia was dead. I was married by then and Ellen and I decided to take the girls in."

"Which brings us back to Milla," Jeffers said, crumpling a napkin and pushing his empty hot dog wrapper to the side.

I surreptitiously tried to draw his attention to a small smear of mustard on his chin.

"Forgive me for rambling," Rodney said, looking down at his uneaten lunch. He took three bites in succession.

"We're in no rush," Jeffers said, oblivious to my subtle hints.

"Sarah was a sweet girl. Always had been. But she'd been forced to grow up too fast. As the older sister, she took it upon herself to take care of Milla when their parents couldn't. When she came to us at eleven, she was already so independent. She and Ellen became very close very quickly. I was worried it might be the other way around—that Sarah would resist Ellen as the matriarch but no. I think Sarah was relieved not to have to do everything anymore. She had moments of real childishness around Ellen. Moments when the little girl she'd had to suppress rose to the surface in desperate need of mothering.

"Milla was the opposite. Sarah had been her everything for so long, so when Sarah turned to Ellen and me, Milla grew resentful. On top of that, I began seeing patterns in her behaviour that reminded me of Jonas as a boy. I knew how my brother's behaviour had nearly destroyed our family and I … overreacted."

"This is the fear and frustration you mentioned?" Jeffers asked.

Rodney nodded. "I didn't want Milla to do what Jonas had done to us. I couldn't let that happen. I personally couldn't go through it again."

"What happened?"

"I forced Milla into therapy. Had her tested for every disorder under the sun. I thought if we could just find out what was causing her behaviour, we could medicate it and everything would be fine."

"Was there ever a diagnosis?"

"No. What Milla needed was the chance to discover herself in the only safe surroundings she'd ever had. She needed space to get to know us—to trust us—on her terms. She needed time. And I didn't see that. I only saw Jonas. I panicked. And I pushed. And I drove her away."

"And you didn't have any contact with her after she left when she was fifteen?"

"No. I looked for her. Every day. I reported her missing when she didn't come home after a few days. I figured with the police looking for her too, we'd have a better chance of finding her…"

"Did she ever make contact with Sarah? Or Ellen?"

Rodney shook his head. "Milla and Sarah grew more and more distant the closer Sarah got to me and Ellen, and she hated Ellen for taking Sarah away from her. They would have told me if she had."

"Did Milla have any friends that you know of?"

"No, she kept to herself. Never had any friends over. Never even talked on the phone."

"She never mentioned any of her classmates?"

"Well ... um ... there was one name that came up a few times. Miranda. I don't have a last name. She was the only person I ever heard Milla talk about and, even then, not a lot. I never met her but Sarah had. I remember Milla being particularly difficult one day and Sarah told us that Miranda and her family had moved, as if that might explain Milla's mood."

"When was this?"

"Just before the girls started high school, I think. I assume they lost touch. I never heard Milla mention her again. Or talk about anyone else. I'm sorry, Detective, I'm not being very helpful."

"On the contrary," Jeffers said. "Understanding Milla's mindset gives us a better idea of where she might have turned when she left." The mustard stain moved up and down as he spoke.

"I failed her, Detective. I took her in and promised to give her the best life I could."

"Your intentions were good," I said. "Everything you did was to help her. She had her reasons for resisting, whether they were founded or not. Sometimes children embrace a new normal, like Sarah, and sometimes they fight it, like Milla."

Like me.

My grandmother, Terri-Mae, had taken me in after my parents died. She had tried, much like Rodney did, to give me normalcy, support, safety. My happiness was her chief concern. And ever elusive. I opposed her at every turn until I, too, finally left. It wasn't my grandmother's fault.

Just like it wasn't Rodney's.

"I feel like I've taken up too much of your time," Rodney said. "You've been very kind. I just wanted to check in. As I said, I feel like I need to do something. I don't want to fail her again."

"Mr. Koepper, I assure you, Milla's case is our top priority. As soon as we have something we can share with you, we will," Jeffers said.

Rodney nodded in understanding but looked disappointed.

"This may have seemed like nothing to you, but everything you've told us today has been very, very helpful. The more we know about Milla—her background—the more we understand her and that, in itself, can provide a number of clues."

Rodney nodded again and even managed a slight smile.

"I won't keep you," he said, rising. "Thank you for seeing me today. It felt surprisingly good to talk about all that. And thank you for lunch."

"Mr. Koepper, we'd like to speak with your wife and Sarah too. They may be able to add to what you've already told us."

"Of course. I'll give you a call with a good time."

"We look forward to hearing from you."

Rodney Koepper nodded his farewell and walked off, carrying his half-eaten hot dog and the weight of the world.

We collected our mess and set off back to the police station.

"You have mustard on your chin."

"What?"

"Mustard. On your chin." I pointed.

"Why didn't you tell me? How long has it been there?"

"I tried to."

"When?"

I repeated all the subtle movements I'd used.

Jeffers stopped. "Is that what you were doing?" He pulled a napkin out the bag that held the remnants of our lunch and wetted it with his tongue. "I thought you had a spasm." He wiped at his chin. "Did I get it?"

The mustard was gone, but the napkin had transferred a smidgeon of ketchup in its place.

I giggled.

"What?"

I overexaggerated my charades from before.

"Very funny," he said.

I shrugged and continued walking.

"I want to talk to Ellen and Sarah and get their take on things. But it sounds to me like there was only one person Milla might have trusted."

"Miranda?"

Jeffers nodded. "We need to track her down."

"Wouldn't the police have done that when Rodney reported Milla missing?"

"Not if Rodney answered the 'friend' question the way he did with me. He didn't mention Miranda until after the second pass."

"But he said they lost touch."

"He said he *assumes* they lost touch. What if they didn't?"

I was catching on. "And what if Miranda was the person Milla ran to?"

"You got it, Samuel. You free for the rest of the day?"

"Isn't that what days off are for?"

Chapter 9

Although it was the summer holiday, the school board's office remained open. A flick of Jeffers' badge and a quick explanation as to what we were looking for got us access to a small office and a computer. One of the administrative staff logged us into the system, entered the passwords necessary to open the student records of the elementary school Milla had attended, and left us alone.

I bent over Jeffers' shoulder as he clicked on the year Milla would have been in grade eight and scrolled down the list of names.

"Miranda Stadler," we said together.

Jeffers typed her name into the search bar of the District School Board of Niagara's mainframe and a screen popped up with her last known address before she'd graduated out of the system.

Jeffers pulled out his phone and sent a quick text to someone at the police station. A ping, moments later, told us the Stadler family was still at that residence.

"We should call first," I said. "We don't even know if she's there. She's twenty-one now. She likely doesn't live at home."

"Don't be so sure. Kids nowadays aren't like you or me. They're perfectly content to live off their parents well into their thirties."

"I guess that means no early retirement for you," I said, referring to his son, Aden, who was still in diapers.

"He has until he finishes university. Then we switch out his mattress for an army cot and Aria cooks only liver and brussels sprouts." I laughed. "Miranda may not be living at home but her family will be able to tell us where to find her. I'd like to avoid too much of a heads-up if we can help it."

"Why? You think Miranda could have something to do with Milla's death?"

"No. But I do think she might have information that could help us and I don't want to risk scaring her off. I'm sure she's seen the news and knows Milla died under suspicious circumstances. If Milla did come to her when she ran away and if Miranda did help in any way, she could be confused as to whether or how she fits into the puzzle."

We returned to the car and began the thirty-minute drive south to the city of Port Colborne.

I'd been to Port Colborne once before. Paul and I had spent a day the previous August taking in the Canal Days Festival, a weekend-long celebration of the region's marine heritage. Buskers, food vendors, artisans, and bands ranging from local acts to nationally known headliners provide entertainment, and everything else one could need, all day and into the evenings.

The highlight for me had been the duck race. On the last day of the festival, numbered rubber ducks are dropped into the canal and are carried by the current to the finish line, their plight detailed by a colour commentary that rivals any coverage heard on the sports network. The winning duck came with a $2500 prize. Sadly, Paul and I did not win.

Paul had been most taken with the tall ships moored in the canal. We'd been able to board and explore several of them, and Paul had been excited to hear that you could take a day-long cruise on one of the vessels from Lake Ontario to Lake Erie through the many locks that linked them. I made a mental note to look into getting tickets this year as a surprise.

Miranda's family lived in a subdivision on the edge of the city. Each house was identical to the one next to it, differentiated only by flower boxes, landscaping, and door decorations. It looked like it would have been brand new when she and her family moved there from St. Catharines years earlier.

Jeffers rang the doorbell several times with no response.

"Can I help you?" a man's voice asked from across the road. He abandoned his lawnmower and moved to stand at the end of his driveway.

"We were hoping to have a word with the Stadlers," Jeffers said. "We'll come back."

"Is everything okay?" he asked, crossing his arms over his chest and adopting a tough-guy stance.

"Oh yes," Jeffers said, smiling.

"You're not selling anything, are you? Or from one of those religious groups?"

"No."

"Then you must be police."

"Why do you say that?" I asked.

"Their daughters are nothing but trouble. The cops are always coming by here. Which one is it this time? Miranda or Tali?"

Jeffers and I exchanged a look.

"Miranda," I said.

"Figures," the neighbour said with a shake of his head. "What'd she do?"

"It's a private matter," Jeffers said. "I'm sure you understand."

The man shrugged and rolled his eyes.

"Do you know where we might find her?" I asked.

"She works at the Y," the neighbour said.

"The YMCA?"

He nodded.

"Thank you very much," Jeffers said.

I offered the man a smile before turning toward the car.

"You could do us all a favour and get those girls off the street," the neighbour called after us. "Before someone gets hurt."

Jeffers gave a polite wave as we drove off. When we'd rounded the corner, he brought the car to a stop and pulled out his phone.

"Go for Steven," the voice on the other end of the line said.

"Steven, it's Jeffers. I—"

"Oh man, you wouldn't believe the hits coming in from your newborn post. Nothing from any of the targets yet, but there's this one guy—"

"Can we hang on to that for a sec? I need to know if Miranda Stadler has a record."

"Stadler with a 'd'?"

"Yes."

I could hear Steven clicking away on a keyboard.

"Nope. No record."

Jeffers and I looked at each other, our faces mirroring the other's confusion.

"You're sure?"

"Not so much as a parking ticket."

"Okay, thanks."

"Right. So anyway," he said, a giggle coming into play, "you're going to love this. There's this guy—"

"Steven, it's going to have to wait. I'll call you when I've finished here."

"Okey-doke," Steven said, disappointment colouring his words, and the call ended.

"So, the neighbour makes Miranda and her sister sound like they're channelling Bonnie Parker, but there's no record?" I said.

"Doesn't mean they're not trouble," Jeffers conceded.

"I guess there's one way to find out."

We found Miranda looking every inch the hardened criminal as she moved through a group of five- and six-year-olds, loosening lids on thermoses, putting straws in juice boxes, and unwrapping granola bars. We'd learned from the front desk that Miranda was the leader of the Junior Explorers camp and that they'd just come in for lunch after a morning digging for worms.

Jeffers tapped on the window of the lunchroom and flashed his badge. I saw Miranda take a deep breath before turning things over to her colleague and excusing herself.

"What have I supposedly done now?" she asked as an amused smile turned up the corners of her mouth.

"I'm sorry?" I asked.

"I'm assuming you're here because Mr. Buckley called you?"

"Mr. Buckley's your neighbour?" Jeffers asked.

"So he did call. Did I slam my car door too loudly this morning when I was leaving for work? Or perhaps he took offence at the colour of my shirt?"

"He didn't call us. But he did tell us where to find you."

Her smile faded and was replaced by a look of concern. "Is everything okay? Has something happened to my parents? Tali?"

"Everyone's fine," Jeffers assured. "Is there somewhere we can talk?"

Miranda led us into a small office across the hall.

"It sounds like you have an ... interesting relationship with Mr. Buckley," Jeffers said.

"At first I was really upset by him. Everything my sister and I do seems to set him off—how close we park to the edge of his driveway, how late we come home and the noise we make, if the dog barks when we walk by his house, if our friends smoke outside—you get the idea. He's called the cops claiming noise violations, trespassing, you name it. The cops eventually stopped coming and my sister and I eventually stopped caring," she said with a laugh. "He's a lonely man. Lost his wife not too long ago. I think he's looking for something to do and someone to talk to more than anything."

"He should get a dog," I said.

"Yeah. So...?" She looked first to me then to Jeffers.

"We're here because we want to talk to you about your relationship with Milla Ward," Jeffers said. "I assume you've seen the news lately?"

Miranda nodded, her expression becoming more serious. "It was quite a shock. We were best friends in elementary school, but I'm sure you already know that or you wouldn't be here." She smiled self-consciously before continuing. "Um ... when my family moved, we didn't see each other much, but we managed to keep in contact. Texting mostly. We lost touch completely a while back, but I always assumed she'd gotten on okay.

"When was the last time you saw her?"

"Oh, gosh. Must have been about four years ago, I think."

"Did you know she'd left home two years before that?"

"Yeah. She didn't get along with her uncle. I don't know if you know that."

Jeffers and I both nodded.

"She told me she was going to leave, which seemed crazy to me. I mean, we were only fifteen. We lost touch after that. I'd heard rumours she was living on the street doing ... all kinds of things. Whatever she needed to do, I guess. I don't really know if that was true. I ran into her sister a couple of times, but she never had any news. Sarah and Milla were never close."

"So you didn't see her when she left?" Jeffers asked. "We thought she might have come to you then."

"No. I didn't think I'd hear from her again, but a couple of years after that I got a message, out of the blue, asking if we could get together."

"Did she say why? After all that time?"

"She was just happy. She told me she met a guy. That she had just moved in with him. She said she still considered me her best friend and wanted me to meet her boyfriend. She said she hoped we could start hanging out again."

"And did you meet?" Jeffers asked.

"Yeah. We had coffee. They drove out here."

"Milla and her boyfriend?"

Miranda nodded.

"How did she seem?"

"I'd never seen her so happy. She looked really ... good. She even said she was going to go home. She wanted to patch things up with her aunt and uncle."

"And did she? Go home?"

Miranda shrugged. "I don't know. I assumed she did. She was really excited about it."

"You didn't speak to her after that?" I asked.

She shook her head. "She said she'd call when she finished putting her spin on the apartment. I messaged her a few times but never heard anything back. I figured she was just busy with moving and everything. It was my grad year so I had a lot going on and, eventually, I kind of forgot about it."

"Did she tell you where the apartment was?"

"Downtown. Above the Sunset restaurant. She said it smelled like bacon," Miranda said with a laugh.

"What about Milla's boyfriend?" Jeffers asked.

"He was older than her. Mid-twenties maybe. Seemed nice."

"Did you get the impression that he was controlling her in any way? Was she at all nervous around him? Fearful?"

"No," Miranda said, shaking her head. "Nothing like that. They looked very much in love."

"Do you remember his name?" I asked.

"Kieran. I remember because I'd never heard that name before."

"Can you tell us anything else about him?"

Miranda gave us a brief physical description before a knock on the window called her back to the group of budding young adventurers.

"I'm sorry. I have to go," she said. "I promised the kids we'd build worm habitats after their snack and I only have them for another hour."

"Of course," Jeffers said. "Here's my card. If you think of anything else about Milla or Kieran, please call."

"I will," she said. Instead of moving to the door, Miranda hesitated. She clearly had something else to say, and I could see her emotions starting to get the better of her. Finally, she said, "Milla had a rough time growing up. But she was really smart and a lot of fun and a good friend and..." Her voice caught in her throat and her eyes started to well up. "Whatever happened, whatever she got herself into ... I'm really glad the last memory I have of her is when she was happy."

Jeffers and I shared a look when Miranda had gone.

"That's not at all what I was expecting," I said.

"Me neither."

"That doesn't sound at all like the Milla Rodney described."

"And Rodney never mentioned seeing Milla again."

"That would mean he lied."

"I don't think that's the case," Jeffers said.

"You don't think she went by like Miranda said?" I asked.

"I think something happened to Milla before she had the chance."

Chapter 10

"Does Jeffers think this Kieran guy has something to do with it?" Paul asked.

"Possibly. He's at the office now trying to track him down," I said.

I'd stopped by the vet clinic with smoothies when Jeffers and I got back from seeing Miranda. I was lucky to catch Paul on a rare break between appointments.

"If he didn't have anything to do with Milla's disappearance," I continued, "chances are he's one of the last people to have seen her before she went missing. Either way, he's someone we need to talk to."

Paul's jaw tightened at my use of the word "we."

I didn't comment on it. Neither did he. There was nothing left in either of our tanks to carry on an argument we'd had countless times. We both knew how it would end.

"Did no one talk to him at the time?"

I shook my head. "No one knew about him. The only person Milla told was Miranda, and she didn't even know

Milla had officially been missing until her body was found. Milla's family didn't know she'd been in contact with Miranda, so there was no reason to question her."

"Well I, for one, have a few questions about why a guy in his mid-twenties is playing house with a seventeen-year-old girl."

"You're not the only one. But an age difference like that isn't nearly as creepy as some of the stuff I saw on the dark web," I said and gave Paul the highlights of my descent into depravity. "Jeffers is coming by later to go over what came in while we were with Miranda."

"I have a meeting when I'm done here, so you guys can chat openly without worrying about how much I can hear when I'm locked away in the kitchen."

"Honey, you're in this too. I need you to be. It doesn't matter what you're supposed to know or how much I'm allowed to tell you."

"It matters to the law."

"But it doesn't matter to me."

"Well, it should. And it has to," Paul said with a smile. He put his smoothie down and wrapped his arms around my waist. "I have to accept my lot as Mr. Emma Samuel."

"That has a nice ring to it," I said, laughing.

"I'm trying," he said, a seriousness joining the smile in his eyes.

"I know."

We stood wrapped in an easy embrace, looking into each other's eyes.

"Is he bringing supper?" Paul asked.

"I don't think so. He didn't mention anything."

"Good. I'll pick up Thai on my way home."

"I like the way you think, Mr. Samuel."

Our kiss was interrupted by a knock on the door. Stephanie, one of the vet techs, stuck her head in.

"Sorry, Paul. I just wanted to let you know that Belinda and Dr. Robertson are here."

"Thank you," Paul said as he let his arms fall from my waist.

"Which one's the patient?" I asked. "Belinda or Dr. Robertson?"

This elicited a chuckle from Paul. "Belinda," he said. "Cat. Poor thing lost her tail last week. A vertebra near the base had been dislocated. Had no choice but to amputate. She's here today so I can see how she's healing."

"How does a cat dislocate her tail?"

"A vertebra," he corrected, "and we're not sure. Her owner found her huddled in a closet with blood on her tail. She spends a lot of time outside, so it's possible she had an incident with a raccoon or fox."

Or an emissary of the devil himself, I thought, as Brimstone sprang to mind.

"Her tail could also have been run over by a bike or stepped on," Paul continued. "Door could have closed on it. You get the idea."

I thought of all the times I had inadvertently stepped on Moustache's tail and vowed to be more mindful. It was near impossible to imagine him without his magnificent plume. Not to mention how much he relied on it for self-expression, conscious or not. I had woken up on many occasions to the sound of it thumping against his bed as he wagged it in his sleep.

I left Paul with a kiss and an order for holy basil chicken with coconut rice and followed the route Stephanie had taken back to the waiting room.

A very distinguished gentleman sat with a tortoiseshell cat in his lap. They both looked intently at the book he was holding. The script on its cover caught my eye.

"What language is that?" I whispered to Stephanie.

"Ancient Greek. Last time he was in, he was reading Latin," she whispered back. As she spoke, her cheeks reddened and her eyes sparkled. She cleared her throat and spoke, breathily, through a smile. "Dr. Robertson, you and Belinda can head back to room two."

"Thank you, Stephanie," Dr. Robertson said in a rich baritone as he tucked the book into his pocket.

Belinda meowed her disapproval, as if she had not finished reading a sentence before the book closed on it. He smiled at us as he made his way into the exam room, and I watched Stephanie's features dissolve into a blush that overtook her entire body.

"He's so handsome" escaped her lips as the door closed behind him, and she lowered her eyes, mortified, when she realized she'd spoken it aloud.

"Yes, he is," I said, hoping to relieve some of her embarrassment.

She smiled shyly and busied herself with some files.

Stephanie was in her early twenties, and I guessed the dashing scholar to be nearing fifty. It was unlikely they would ever strike up a romance, but it got me thinking about the age difference between Milla Ward and her boyfriend.

The illustrious "they" say the biggest obstacle to the success of relationships with significant age gaps is the fact that the parties are at different emotional, economic, and social stages in life. A better example couldn't have been a twenty-something guy with his own apartment and, presumably, some kind of regular employment and a teenage runaway who'd spent time living on the street.

"Kieran Martin is still at the apartment," Jeffers said when he stopped by later. "I haven't had a chance to interview him yet. I spent most of the afternoon weeding through the responses to my post."

"Anything promising?"

"We've flagged one as a possibility. I've let Steven take over the conversation for the time being. My stomach can't bear it. I'll spare you the details. Trust me."

"It can't be that bad. I mean, yes, selling babies is bad, but presumably they're being sold to people who will go on to love them and give them happy lives and … what?"

"That's not the only reason they're being sold."

"What do you mean?" The second the question had passed my lips, I was sorry I'd asked it. From the look on Jeffers' face, I knew I didn't want to know the answer.

"There's this one guy—"

"Never mind," I said, before he could continue. "I'm going to stick with my own belief that the only intentions are good ones."

"Good idea. And while you're at it, perhaps you can put a rosy spin on what a twenty-six-year-old man would want from a seventeen-year-old girl."

"You sound like Paul. Hopefully, Kieran can do that for us when we speak with him."

Jeffers smiled. The opposite reaction to the one Paul had had when I'd included myself in official business.

"How's tomorrow?" he asked.

"I have a matinee. After that, I'm good."

"Great. In the meantime, we can get started on these," he said, dropping the stack of files Lindsey had given us earlier onto the coffee table with a loud thwack.

The noise woke Moustache, who was splayed on the floor by the front door trying to keep cool on the tiles. He raised his head just enough to sniff the air and, after determining that whatever had made the noise wasn't worth more extensive exploration, lowered his head with a snort.

"These are the businesses that could be covers for the baby ring," Jeffers said.

I started flipping through the files. There were a couple of transitional residential homes for homeless or at-risk young women aged sixteen to eighteen, aimed at reintegrating them into society through educational and social programs. One was in St. Catharines, another in Niagara Falls.

"You think whoever's involved is preying on pregnant teenagers?"

"It makes sense. Pregnant young girls would be offered a lot of money to carry their babies to term rather than abort. Here they have a place to stay during their pregnancies and, if they like the money, there's a chance they can be persuaded to become surrogates for the bigger operation. Otherwise, they sell their baby, take the money, and run. It's a win-win for them."

"They're probably not being paid even close to the amount of money the people in charge are getting for selling the babies."

"Definitely not."

A third file bore the name of a St. Catharines soup kitchen.

"Again, preying on women who've fallen on hard times. Nutritious meals, supplies, emergency shelter. Exactly what a pregnant woman needs. Throw some money into the mix and the deal gets even sweeter," I said.

"That's also the last place Angela Hansen was seen alive," Jeffers said.

"What?"

"A few days after she went missing, one of the volunteers recognized Angela's picture on the news and called the police. He said she'd come in a couple of days earlier with a group of regulars, and the reason she stood out was that she was cleaner than the rest. Other than that, he took no further notice of her."

"Were the police able to find the people she came in with?"

"Yeah. They were all questioned. Apparently, Angela had stumbled upon their little camp by the Burgoyne Bridge."

"That's not far from the radio station."

"They were heading over to the soup kitchen for lunch and asked Angela if she wanted to join them. They all said she wasn't making much sense and they had a feeling something was wrong. Figured they'd keep her close and eventually someone would come looking for her."

"Well, they didn't do a very good job."

"No. One of the guys said she wandered off in the direction of the bathroom once they got their lunches. When she didn't come back, they all thought she'd taken off. Didn't give it another thought."

"And no one else at the soup kitchen remembers seeing her?"

"Not according to her file. I went through the transcripts of all the interviews hoping to find something but…" He shook his head.

"Something must have happened in the bathroom."

"Yeah. She vanished into thin air."

"Is this place under suspicion for other reasons or just because it was the last place Angela was seen?"

"The latter. But that's a good enough reason as any."

The last few folders held information on an organization called The Family Circle, and the name and details of two private adoption practitioners.

"What do they do?" I asked.

"They work with prospective applicants to make sure all the paperwork is complete and accounted for. They are also approved to do home studies and supervise placements."

"Approved by whom?"

"The government."

"It wouldn't be the first time a government agency has been involved in dirty dealings."

Jeffers laughed. "I doubt very much that the Ministry of Children, Community, and Whatever It Is has any idea what these two might be up to. I can almost guarantee it."

"*If* they're up to something," I said.

"They're definitely up to something. We just don't know what the something is."

The Family Circle was a private adoption agency also located in Niagara Falls and also licensed by the government.

"Okay," I said. "So, you and Lindsey think the people working for these organizations have something to do with the baby ring?"

"Not all the organizations and certainly not all the people. But Lindsey and her team have flagged these groups as suspicious based on a very lengthy investigation. We have every reason to believe that someone associated with one of these groups is a member of a much larger operation."

"Ah, it's the old needle in a haystack thing," I said.

Jeffers nodded. "The good news is it's not a big haystack."

"I still don't see why they need you," Paul said, moving a container of spring rolls out of Moustache's reach.

Moustache had both paws up on the kitchen island and was stretching his snout and tongue as far as they would go toward where he last knew the appetizers to be. Foiled but not defeated, he dropped to all fours and quickly moved to the other side of the island and resumed his Stretch Armstrong impression. He succeeded in licking the outside of the container before my hand came down on the lid, crushing his dreams. His focus shifted to the counter where Paul was portioning rice into ceramic bowls.

"They want me apprised on all parts of the investigation in case avenues overlap. And it's my job to connect with the adoption practitioners," I said. "I have appointments with two the day after tomorrow."

"To pose as a wishful, would-be mom?"

"Yep. Desperate enough to buy a baby on the black market."

"You can't just go in there and say you want to buy a baby."

"Well, of course not," I said, removing the lid from my chicken dish and letting the spices tickle my nostrils. "I have to be rejected for a traditional adoption first. I told you that."

"Yes," Paul said, spooning panang curry over his rice. "And how are you going to orchestrate that?"

"What?" I asked.

"Your ineligibility for an adoption. You told me all the reasons why people might be rejected, so ... what's yours?"

As my brain stumbled around my head looking for an answer, I fumbled the lid to the satay sauce and sent it tumbling to floor, where an eager Moustache wasted no time in licking it clean. The mishap gave me the perfect excuse not to answer and, after escorting the dog to the backyard, I made a hasty retreat to the bathroom to make a frantic call to Jeffers.

"Surely you've done something bad," Jeffers said.

"Not unless you count shutting everyone out of my life for years and behaving like a general brat. I told you in Morris' office that I'm an ideal candidate."

"There's got to be something shady. If not, make it up. You're an actor."

"That's not how it works and you know it."

"Relax, Samuel. I'm kidding."

"I can't believe we forgot about this," I said. "This is a significant detail. This is what gets us through the hidden door."

"*We* didn't forget about it. *You're* just getting ahead of yourself. There are a lot of hoops to go through before we get to that. You're just making contact first—gathering information on the adoption process, getting a feel for the practitioner, learning about the home study—all that stuff. Focus on your need for privacy and your desire for a baby. Get them to like you and see what a great mother you'll be. That way when we do finally work in something damaging, they'll be more inclined to want to help you."

"Okay. Sorry," I said, taking a deep breath. "I just…"

"Panicked?"

"Yeah. I really want to catch these people."

"I know. Me too. Lindsey and I will make sure you're covered when the time comes. And if worse comes to worse, we'll just add Paul to the mix."

"What do you mean, 'add Paul'?"

"We'll bring him in on this. If he's okay with that."

"I don't see how he could help."

"Well, he does have a criminal record."

Chapter 11

Paul was standing in the hallway when I opened the door.

"Jeffers just texted me. He thought you knew."

"Why *don't* I know?"

"I—"

"Is it true?"

"If you come into the living room, I'll explain everything over supper."

"I don't care about supper."

My mind was reeling. Paul and I had been together for almost two years. There was good, bad, and ugly on both sides, and I thought we had shared it all with each other.

It hadn't been easy for me to open myself up so completely. Apart from Natalie and Jeffers, I hadn't allowed myself to trust anyone as unconditionally as I did Paul and his omission of such a huge detail felt like a betrayal.

"Bells, you're making this a bigger thing than it is."

"Am I? You have a criminal record. That means you weren't just arrested for a minor shenanigan like smuggling someone into the drive-in or stealing a chocolate bar from the drugstore. You weren't a little boy the police were trying to scare. You have a record. A record!"

Paul nodded.

"When were you going to tell me? What if we wanted to take a trip? You can't leave the country."

"I know that and I—"

"And what about—"

"Bells, stop!"

I had never heard Paul raise his voice. It sounded louder in the narrow hallway than it would have in a bigger space, but it still achieved what he wanted.

"I will explain everything to you if you just come and sit down."

I petulantly folded my arms across my chest and refused to move.

"Fine," he said and sat on the floor with his back against the wall and his legs outstretched. "There was a protest at the marine park a few years ago. It had been planned and organized and was peaceful for all intents and purposes."

"What was the protest about?"

"A former trainer at the park had made allegations about animal abuse."

It was becoming clear to me. And I felt like a fool. I didn't know what I'd been expecting Paul to say or why I assumed it would be something horrible. He simply didn't have it in him to do something heinous. I knew that. And, yet, I had still allowed myself to fly off the handle and allow every worst-case scenario to play itself out in my mind.

"Of course you'd want to be there," I said. "I'm sorry. I totally overreacted. Although I do think a criminal record is a little harsh for a protesting arrest."

"There was a little more to it than that," Paul sheepishly admitted.

"Oh?"

"I did go to the protest. And I heard a lot about what was apparently going on inside the park—complaints about the animals' living conditions, improper medical care, instances of starvation and isolation. I was enraged, as you can imagine. Especially since I knew some of the veterinary staff there. I couldn't believe they would allow the things that were being alleged. I was horrified.

"I was there with my buddy, Jens, who was the other vet with me at the clinic then, and a friend of his who happened to be some kind of computer genius, and the three of us came up with a crazy, stupid idea to break into the office at night, access all the vet records, and leak them to several news outlets."

"Oh my god!"

"We were caught by one of the security guards, who called the police, and yada yada yada."

"Didn't one of you stand lookout?"

Paul laughed. "Didn't even occur to us. None of us were professional criminals, see. We were just animal lovers."

"So what happened?"

"We were charged with breaking and entering with the intent to commit an offence therein. Also, with theft of property under five thousand dollars."

My eyes widened. "Granted, my knowledge of the law is primarily from *Port Authority*, but isn't breaking and entering indictable?"

"It is. With a sentence of ten years. Theft under five thousand can be either an indictable or a summary offence with a sentence of only six months or a fine."

"And you said it wasn't a big deal."

"Well—"

"What are you even doing here? How did you get off?"

I knew I was being irrational and overreacting. The fact that Paul was sitting on the floor in my hallway and had, for as long as I'd known him, been living a free life as an upstanding citizen should have alleviated the panic I could feel grabbing hold of my innards, but it didn't, and I began to shake.

"Bells, come here," he said, reaching out his arm to me.

I sat down next to him and settled into the crook of his elbow.

"When the papers got hold of the records and published their stories, it became clear that none of the animals had suffered any physical abuse and were all in reasonably good health."

"Reasonably?"

"Yes. There was some evidence of malnutrition and environmental injuries and a few other things. Basically, there was enough information to dispel the serious allegations that had been made but not enough to force an investigation. In the end, the park was cleared of any negligence but was required to make improvements to the habitats and bring in consultants to redesign the feeding regimens. Despite the debate over life in captivity, I'm happy to say all of the animals have been receiving better care and living better lives ever since."

"Are you saying you're a hero then?"

"Well, I don't have a cape or anything…"

I smiled and he pulled me closer to him.

"That still doesn't explain why you're not in jail."

"I was. For one night and the better part of a morning."

"But they didn't keep you there."

"No. We were all pretty good guys. These were our first brushes with the law, so to speak, and, thankfully, the judge was able to recognize we weren't out to do any harm even though what we did was incredibly stupid. He dropped both charges to summary offences and fined us all a good chunk of change."

"But you still have a record."

"For another couple of years. Then I can apply for a pardon."

I took a deep breath as my mind started to process everything.

"I'm sorry," Paul said. "I know this is a lot. I should have told you. I wasn't hiding it from you—I just honestly don't think about it. How did this all come up, anyway?"

"Jeffers thinks you might be able to help us with the adoption case."

"Really?"

He had answered quickly. Too quickly. I turned and looked him square in the face and saw an excited twinkle in his eye. I decided to have a little fun.

"But I told Jeffers it was out of the question."

"What?"

"I know how you feel about me working with him—it's far too dangerous and police work should be left to the police…"

"Well, yeah, but—"

"I mean, we've had countless arguments about this," I said, talking over him. "And I love you and respect you and that's why I knew how you'd react, so I told Jeffers it would be better to leave things as they are and keep you out of it."

He stared at me, speechless.

"You've made your position very clear," I said. "And I know there's nothing I could ever say to convince you to help."

"Bells—"

"It's okay. Jeffers gets it. We'll figure something else out."

Moustache scratched at the back door wanting to be let in.

"Come on," I said getting to my feet. "Let's eat."

I gave Paul's shoulder a squeeze and stepped around the corner.

"I want to be a Hardy Boy," he said quietly.

I poked my head back into the hallway. "Sorry?"

He was still sitting on the floor and refused to meet my gaze.

"I know what I said. And I do feel those things and if I had my way neither of us would be anywhere near stuff like this. But you are. And because you are, I am, and since I am then I'd rather be in the game than watching, helplessly, from the sidelines."

He looked up at me with an expression he could only have copied from one of the puppies in his care, and I steeled myself against its power, determined to keep up the ruse.

"Bells, please," he said, moving from his seat to knees. "I know you think I'm a hypocrite and I suppose I am, but I can't get that baby out of my mind and if I can do anything to—"

"Frank or Joe?"

"What?"

"Which Hardy Boy do you want to be?"

"Well, Frank is the more logical of the two, but given that Joe was the one of who landed behind bars, I guess, by default…"

By this point all my anger had gone and my energy to continue the charade of keeping Paul away from the investigation followed suit. My stomach was growling, Moustache was still scratching at the back door, and I found myself unable to keep a straight face.

"What?" Paul asked as he saw my expression.

"I'm impressed by the depth of your Hardy Boys knowledge. I couldn't tell you if it was Shaun or David Cassidy who played one in the TV series let alone that Joe went to jail."

"It was Shaun. He played Joe. Parker Stevenson played Frank." Paul said, getting to his feet. He draped an arm around my shoulders and led me to the kitchen. "And Joe didn't really go to jail. He just locked himself in a cell so an assassin couldn't catch him."

"Oooo, and then what happened?" I asked as I opened the back door and Moustache came hurtling through.

"The assassin shot him."

"Well, yeah, I guess it wasn't really well thought out. I mean, you're behind bars, not a solid wall. Sounds like Joe wasn't all that bright. Maybe you should reconsider and be Frank."

Paul's phone chirped.

"It's Jeffers," he said, reading the text. "He wants to know if you freaked out and if everything's okay. What should I tell him?"

"Tell him everything is fine," I said.

Paul started thumbing a response.

"And tell him that I'd love to have you help us."

Paul smiled as he wrote that part.

"But don't tell him he's Joe. He may not take kindly to being the dumb one."

"Okay," Paul said, laughing.

I stuck my bowl of Thai take-out into the microwave and added as an afterthought, "And ask him why he ran a background check on my boyfriend."

"I was just looking out for you," Jeffers told me over the phone the next day. "You hadn't been involved with anyone for a while, and I wanted to make sure he was good enough for you before you got too far in. I needed peace of mind."

"Why didn't you ever tell me?"

"Because I didn't want you to *know* I was looking out for you." I could tell he was grinning by the way his words came out. "Anyway, it's not like he's a real criminal. And this is good, right? This is perfect for the adoption people. If I'd told you sooner, who knows what might have happened? Now you're too much in love to let this come between you. Let's face it, I may have actually ensured relationship success by keeping quiet."

I rolled my eyes and stepped through the stage door in time to see Sean Maffey trip up the stairs and almost drop the stack of binders he was carrying. He managed to get a handle on them before they fell, but in doing so poked himself in the eye with the straw that was sticking out of the top of the iced cappuccino he had nestled in his elbow.

"Jeffers, I have to go," I said.

"Okay. I'll pick you up after your show. Kieran gets off work at four thirty and should be home. And Rodney Koepper called to say it's a good evening for us to stop by to talk to Sarah and Ellen. You got time?"

"Yep. See you in a bit."

We hung up and I moved to help a struggling Sean.

"Oh, that's okay, Bella, thanks," he said, completely unfazed and looking at me through his one good eye. His other was squeezed tightly shut and tears flowed freely down his cheek.

"Give me the binders," I insisted.

He handed the stack off to me and immediately began rubbing his eye with his free hand.

"What are all these?" I asked, barely able to see over the top of them.

"Scripts for the directors' projects."

Each year, the Shaw hires two emerging directors to take part in the season. They each act as an assistant director on a couple of productions while helming their own one-act play that is performed as part of a special showcase in the fall.

Ginny Lao, one of the interns who had worked with us on *Quality Street*, had asked me to be in hers. I liked her quite a bit, and she seemed to have a head full of good ideas, so I said I'd be happy to take on a small role. At the time, she had still been in the process of choosing a play and getting it approved and, while there had been rumblings, no one knew for certain which plays had finally been given the go-ahead. Neither the plays nor the casting would be revealed for another week or two—just prior to the August rehearsals. I was hoping for something dramatic as my funny bone was already being worked to the hilt this season.

"Oh, they've been decided, then?"

"Yes. And no peeking. I've got to get these to the production office."

Sean picked up the pace, and I followed as best I could. With Sean's one eye and my vision obscured by a mountain of binders, we truly were the blind leading the blind.

We rounded a corner and Sean walked straight into Jarod Riley and I walked straight into Sean. This time the straw went up Sean's nose, making him yelp.

"God, these things should come with a warning label," Sean said with a laugh.

"Let me help," Jarod said, relieving me of half the binders, and together the three of us continued our journey.

"What's all this?" Jarod asked.

"Directors' project scripts," I said.

"Oooh."

"No peeking," Sean said from the head of the pack.

"Are you doing one of these?" Jarod asked.

"I am," I said and instantly regretted it when I saw him perk up.

"Me too. The universe keeps throwing us together this season," he said with a wink. "I'm excited. Matt was throwing around some really interesting titles so we should have a good time."

"Oh," I said, trying to keep the euphoria out of my voice and off my face. "I'm doing Ginny's, not Matt's. Guess the universe has other plans."

"Hmmm," he said, but the look on his face made me wonder what his mind was up to.

We arrived at the production office and deposited the scripts. Sean stuffed a tissue up his nose to stop the small trickle of blood that had started and hurried off to prep for our matinee. I mumbled something about caffeine and headed toward the green room. When Jarod started to accompany me, I pretended that my phone had vibrated and excused myself to take the call.

I was surprised to find Adam using the back stairs.

"What are you doing here?" I asked. "Don't you have a show?"

Our schedules were almost identical in spite of the fact we were only in the one show together. Adam's second show ran at almost always the same time as *Arms and the Man*.

"I'm not in until the second act, so now that we're up and running, the stage manager said I didn't have to come in until the show started."

"Bully for you."

"I know, right. Small perks. Anyway, I was looking for you. I wanted to give you this."

He pulled a pamphlet out of his bag and handed it to me.

"Oops, not that," he said, snatching the pamphlet back and replacing it with a bedazzled envelope. He stuffed the pamphlet back into his bag.

"What was that?" I asked.

"That? Nothing. But this…" He said, tapping on the envelope in my hand.

"Are you and Powell thinking of adopting a baby?"

"What? What would give you that idea? Look," he said, taking the envelope from me and waving it in front of my face while making oohing sounds. I grabbed the envelope out of his hand.

"I saw the pamphlet."

"I don't see a pamphlet. Now just—"

"Adam."

"Okay, yes. But you weren't supposed to see that. No one is supposed to know. We're just … never mind … shh."

"I didn't realize you guys were that serious," I said.

"Well, if you'd open the damn envelope…"

I worked my way through the glitter and gems and pulled out a glossy picture of two male models in Armani suits with the heads of Adam and Powell superimposed onto their well-dressed bodies along with the words "You're Invited!" I flipped the picture over to see all the details of their August wedding.

I squealed and clapped and drew Adam in for a hug.

"I know some people think it's too soon," he said.

"Well, it is just a few weeks away."

"Not the wedding. The marriage. We've only been together a year. But we don't care. We're in love, and we're doing this. I'm thinking of copying the tuxedo gown Billy Porter wore to the Oscars that one year. Maybe not with such a full skirt. I like a sleeker line, but we'll see. Powell's doing a traditional tux. You know how he is."

Adam was bursting with enthusiasm. Positively glowing. The smile on my face stretched as wide as his. I was absolutely delighted for both of them.

"So, a wedding and a baby?" I asked.

"Well, we want to do it all, and Powell is going to be fifty in January. He doesn't want to be an old dad and—"

"Powell is going to be fifty?"

"I know, right? I had him show me five pieces of ID before I believed him."

Powell Avery had starred opposite me in Cabaret the season before. He easily surpassed the criteria for tall, dark, and handsome. A classic Hollywood leading man who would rival Cary Grant or Clark Gable. I would have put him in his early forties at the latest and fully believed he could convincingly play someone in their mid-thirties if the theatre was big enough.

"Anyway," Adam said, "adoptions take time and we want to get the ball rolling. Please don't say anything to anyone."

"I won't."

"And please tell me you'll come. And that you'll be a bridesmaid."

"Not if I have to wear seafoam taffeta."

Adam brought his hand to his heart as if I'd wielded a mortal blow. "My god, woman, what do you take me for? I will let nothing upstage the bride. Especially bad fashion."

"I'm kidding. And I wouldn't miss it."

"And you'll bring Paul, of course. Maybe you guys will even catch the bouquet."

"You keep your wedding fever to yourself," I said. "We're not heading down that road."

Chapter 12

"Oh, before I forget," Jeffers said, throwing a ziplock bag containing several gold bands onto my lap. We were en route to see Kieran after my matinee. "Now that Paul's involved, Lindsey wants to expedite things. She wants you to mention the criminal record early on. See what kind of reaction it gets and whether the avenue is worth pursuing from our end. She already knows these organizations are into something, and she wants to be sure it's the right something before we get too far in. I think she's worried there might be more victims if we don't hurry."

"That's certainly a valid concern," I said. "What are these for?"

"Lindsey also said it would be better for you two to be 'married.'"

"So, a corrupt adoption practitioner has no trouble selling babies illegally but is going to play the morality card and only sell to married couples? That makes no sense," I said.

"It's not that. If you two aren't married, the practitioner could still authorize an adoption for you as a single woman and, therefore, Paul's record becomes moot as does the need for anything underhanded. You see where I'm going with this?"

I nodded. "Paul's criminal record is the key to the door of the underworld. I need to be ineligible by association."

"Yep. So, by the power vested in me…"

I looked at the array of rings in my lap. Yellow gold. Not my favourite. They all boasted a few scuffs, and it looked like there had been inscriptions on a couple of them at one time, but they were illegible due to wear. They were all different—one had a beveled edge, one a hammered finish. I didn't know if it was a good or bad thing that there wasn't a matching set.

"I wasn't sure of your sizes so I grabbed a bunch," Jeffers said.

"I don't even get a rock?" I asked.

"We don't have that many, and the ones we do have we keep for deep cover. If you really want one, maybe Paul will get one for you," he said with a smirk.

"This will be fine," I said pointedly and looked out the window, hoping to discourage any further talk on the matter.

"You guys ever talk about it?" Jeffers asked.

"No."

"Is it something—"

"Jeffers!"

"What? You guys have been together for a while now. It's not an unreasonable question."

"We haven't talked about it. I don't want to talk about it. Everything is perfectly fine just the way it is."

"Okay," he said, and a merciful silence ensued for a handful of seconds before Jeffers broke in again. "I'm just saying you guys seem really solid and it's nice seeing you happy. I think it would be really great for you."

"For me?"

"For him too. But especially you."

"Why's that?" I asked, trying to keep my voice calm and my breathing steady.

I didn't know why my go-to reaction was one of irritation whenever someone brought up the idea of us getting married. Natalie had started the ball of indignation rolling several months prior by bringing up the idea during one of our phone calls. It had picked up steam when Adam mentioned the bouquet and was gaining in momentum as this conversation continued.

"I just think you're ready to have a family again," he said. "I don't mean kids or anything like that. Not that you shouldn't have kids, if you want them."

"I have a family."

"Who? Moustache?"

"Yes. And Natalie. And y—" I stopped myself before I included Jeffers. I wasn't sure I wanted to include him anymore until I saw where this discussion ended up.

"You know what I mean."

As much as I didn't want to admit it, I did know what he meant. After all my years of pushing people away for fear of losing them like I did my parents, my frozen heart had begun to thaw bit by bit. First with Natalie, then Moustache, then Jeffers, and Adam, and finally Paul.

Unbeknownst to Jeffers, the ball of indignation came to a screeching halt moments before it would have flattened him completely. And in that moment, I realized I didn't seize up at the mention of marriage because I feared commitment or was unable to experience love. It was the opposite. The truth was, the subject had never once come up between Paul and me. Not even as a joke. And I worried that ever after was something he didn't see when he looked at me.

A car pulled out of a spot right in front of the Sunset restaurant and Jeffers executed a perfect parallel park to take over the space. Kieran's apartment was at the top of a narrow flight of stairs. He opened the door almost immediately after we'd knocked.

"Oh," he said upon seeing us. "I'm sorry, I was expecting—"

"Sorry, man," a thirty-something hipster said as he came through the off-street entrance and began climbing the stairs. "Some dude scooped the parking space right out front and I had to go around. But I brought the stuff." He proudly held a bag aloft.

By this time, he'd reached the steps just below the landing on which Jeffers and I were standing and finally registered our presence.

"Oh."

"Perhaps we should introduce ourselves," Jeffers said, holding out his badge. "I'm the dude who scooped your parking space, and this is my partner. We were hoping to have a quick word with Mr. Martin here."

"This isn't…" the hipster said, indicating the bag. "I mean, it's not…"

"Even if it is, that's not why we're here," Jeffers said.

"Well, it isn't," Kieran said, taking the bag. "And please come in."

He shot a look at his buddy, who quickly retreated the way he'd come.

"What is this about?" Kieran asked, shutting the door behind him and placing the bag, unopened, on a small table by the front door.

"Milla Ward," Jeffers said.

Kieran's mouth fell open in surprise but he said nothing.

"You had a relationship with Miss Ward, did you not?"

"Yes. But how did you know that? No one knew that."

"Was it a secret?"

"No. Not at all. It's just that we didn't really know anyone and … it doesn't matter. What can I do for you?"

"We spoke with her friend, Miranda."

"Right," Kieran said and nodded his head as if the memory had just been dislodged from the far recesses of his brain.

"I assume you've seen the news," Jeffers said.

Kieran nodded and motioned to the living room where we all made ourselves a little more comfortable.

"I don't suppose you know what happened," Kieran said.

"Not yet," said Jeffers, "We're still putting the pieces together. We're hoping you might be able to help with that."

"Whatever I can do. Can I get you anything? Lemonade? I just made some." He got up and made his way to a little galley kitchen.

The apartment was small and open, neatly kept, and nicely decorated despite a stack of cardboard boxes in the hall that led, presumably, to the bedroom.

"From scratch?" I asked.

"Of course."

"Oh," I said, a little taken aback. I'd been expecting something from a mix.

"Don't be alarmed," he said as he poured a mossy-green liquid into three glasses. "I make it with cilantro."

Jeffers and I exchanged a look. Kieran laughed.

"Cilantro has been used for ages as a digestive aid. It also supports liver function and is an excellent anti-inflammatory. On top of all that, it has a natural cooling effect and helps to relieve heat in the body. With the weather we've been having, I always have a jug in the fridge. Can't help but bring my work home with me." He chuckled at his own joke.

"What do you do?" I asked.

"I'm a registered medical herbalist."

"A what?"

"I treat people with health issues using plant medicine. And this, in case you're wondering," he said, pointing to the mystery bag, "is full of more cilantro and some other herbs. I like to grow whatever I can myself. My cousin, the guy who was here, and his wife have a farm and let me use a small area."

He set two glasses in front of Jeffers and me and took a long swallow from his own.

I took a polite, tentative sip. It was delicious. Despite my saying so to Jeffers, he left his glass untouched.

"Mr. Martin, when was the last time you saw Milla?"

"Four years ago. April 17 at eight twenty in the morning."

"That's awfully specific," Jeffers said.

"People either tend to remember exactly where they were, what they were doing, and when they were doing it when something traumatic happens or they don't remember anything at all," Kieran said. "Milla and I were here in the apartment. We had just had breakfast and I was leaving for an early class. She was about to get into the shower."

"Do you know what her plans were for that day?"

"She had a job interview later that afternoon. She was nervous about it."

"Do you happen to remember what time her interview was?"

Kieran shook his head. "One or two, maybe. I can't remember exactly. It was for a cashier position at Costco. She called me after and said it went really well. She was very excited."

Jeffers made a note. "Did she say anything else?"

"She said she was going to go by her aunt and uncle's place. I'm assuming you know they had a difficult relationship."

Jeffers and I nodded.

"She and I had talked about it a lot. And I knew she wanted to wait until she was really ready before she went to see them. Until she really had herself together, I mean. I was a little surprised when she said she was going to see them that day, but she told me she just felt it was the right time. That the interview had given her the boost she needed.

"I was happy for her. This was such a huge step in her recovery. I told her I'd pick up something special for supper and we'd celebrate."

"What do you mean by recovery? Were you treating her?" I asked.

"No. I was still in school then. I was finishing my master's degree at Brock. But I did get her in to see a counsellor. She was really serious about getting her life back on track and about making amends."

"How did you two meet?"

The more he talked, the less I could imagine them together. The curiosity was killing me.

He laughed. "She was begging outside the restaurant downstairs. I'd see her every morning when I left for class. I always made sure I had some change in my pocket. Eventually, I added some small talk to the change and then one day I asked if I could get her a meal. I could see she was in a bad way. I wanted to help."

"And how did you go from sharing a meal to living together?" Jeffers asked. "That's kind of over and above, don't you think?"

"We just hit it off. I can't explain it. It wasn't like anything I'd experienced before."

"You just hit it off?" Jeffers said.

"Yeah," he said, smiling at the memory.

"What could a twenty-five-year-old master's degree candidate possibly have in common with a fifteen-year-old street kid?"

"She was sixteen when we met, and please don't imply that I took advantage because it wasn't—"

"But you did take advantage. Yours was a relationship built on dependency—she on you—and given the age difference between you, that calls into question the age of consent," Jeffers argued.

"Don't do that. Please," Kieran said. "I loved her. We loved each other."

"An adult and a teenager have very different ideas of what love is."

"Jeffers," I said quietly. And it was all I need to say.

Kieran looked more hurt than angry, but I worried that, should the balance tip, we would lose our chance to put this part of the puzzle together.

"Tell us about her," I said, hoping to calm Kieran. "We've spoken with her family, of course, but we'd love to get to know the Milla you knew."

I saw some of the tension leave Kieran's body. But not all. It was obvious to me that he wanted to trust us and wanted to help, but he'd put his guard up against Jeffers' insinuations. I was sure if I could get him talking again, those defences would come down.

"She was sixteen, yes," he started, "but living on your own on the street forces you to grow up fast. She seemed older than her years. She … I don't know how to put this … she had this natural wisdom, I guess you could say. This way of looking at the world that was just … I don't know … refreshing."

"What do you mean?"

"She'd had a hard life but she never used that as an excuse. It was always something that drove her. Fuelled her. It was what made her get back up and keep fighting and dreaming. God, she had dreams. Big ones. We were going to…

"Detective, I know it's hard for you to believe that people from completely different worlds could come together, but we did. We worked. And not because she needed anything from me but because I listened, and cared, and allowed her to be herself in all her wonderful glory. That's all I ever wanted for her. And from her."

"And what about you?" Jeffers asked. "What did you get out of it?"

"I've never had an easy time making friends outside of school. Especially girlfriends. I mean, look at me."

Kieran was nerdy, it was true. And not a cute nerdy like the kind who takes off his glasses and turns into a heartthrob. He was nerdy through and through. But there was a charm to his geekiness, and I imagined that's what might have drawn Milla to him. My guess was that she felt safe with him.

"I never know what to say to girls. I always end up going off on some botanical tangent that's so boring that even I lose interest in what I'm talking about," he said with a laugh. "My dad died when I was young, and my mom never felt I was man enough to be the man of the house. She would look at me, trying to find some remnant of my father, but she couldn't. I can't tell you how many times she told me how glad she was he had died so that he didn't have to see what I turned into. The ironic thing was that I was much more like my dad than any of my siblings, even if I didn't look like it.

"Anyway, I think Milla and I bonded, initially, over difficulties in our family lives. But then it grew into something deeper. She never seemed bored when I'd rattle on about plants and herbs. She said it was cute. She liked that I was so passionate about something. I never felt embarrassed about who I was when I was with her."

Jeffers reached out for his glass of lemonade but seemed to think better of it and leaned back in his seat.

"Can you tell us what happened when Milla didn't come home that night?" Jeffers asked, fanning himself with his notebook. His tone had softened somewhat.

"She wasn't here when I got back from school. I took that as a good sign—that things had gone well with her family. But it got later and later, and she wasn't answering any of my texts. I tried calling too, but it went right to voice mail. I didn't know what to do. I didn't know where her aunt and uncle lived, so I couldn't even go over there. I was frantic. But all I could do was wait."

"You didn't think of going to the police?" I asked.

"I was going to go the next day. But she called."

"What did she say?"

"It was weird. It was her voice, but it wasn't her, if that makes any sense. She was cold and distant, and she said it had been a mistake being with me, that it was over between us and that she didn't want me to contact her again."

"That was it?"

Kieran nodded. "I didn't understand. I couldn't. The day before she had been so excited. About everything. She told me she loved me. I tried calling her back, but she must have blocked my number or something because the call wouldn't go through."

I looked at Jeffers. He was writing something in his notebook.

"And that was the last time you heard from her?" Jeffers asked, his eyes intent on whatever he was writing.

"No."

Jeffers head shot up.

"She called about a year ago. She phoned the clinic where I work. I don't know how she even knew about it. It had only been open for a couple of months. I wasn't there at the time. She must have called after we'd closed for the day. I got the message as soon as I got in the next morning."

"And?"

"I could barely understand her. The signal kept cutting out. She was crying, and it was obvious she was trying to be quiet. Like she didn't want anyone else to hear. She was also slurring her words. Like she was having trouble speaking. I think she was asking for help, but I wasn't sure."

"And you're sure it was her?" I asked.

Kieran nodded.

"Did you call her back?" Jeffers asked.

"Of course. It went to voice mail. Someone named Keesha. I left a message. No one ever called me back. I've never gotten an answer all the times I've tried, and I've tried every day since."

"Still?" I asked. "It's been months."

Kieran shrugged.

"Did you save the message?"

"Yes, well, no. Messages are automatically deleted after a certain period of time. I had saved it repeatedly, and then one day it was gone."

Jeffers chewed on the end of his pen, taking this all in. "I'm going to need you to give me that number," he said finally.

"Sure." Kieran took out his phone, swiped a few times, and then read out the digits, which Jeffers copied into his notebook.

"Are you moving?" I asked. "I saw boxes in the hallway."

Kieran nodded. "Once I heard the news … Not much point in staying. I only kept this apartment so Milla would be able to find me. If she wanted."

"Even though she told you it was over?"

Kieran smiled, embarrassed. "Guess that makes me kind of pathetic, huh?"

"Where are you moving?" Jeffers asked.

"I bought a property in Vineland a few years back but never made the move out. It's more house than I need but the land is good and that's my main concern. Now that I'm going to be out there full-time, I can get the ground ready to relocate the plants my cousin has and get some new seeds in the ground. It will help me build a better relationship with my herbs. I might even open my own practice."

"Do you mind giving us the address? In case we need to speak with you again," Jeffers said.

"The house isn't in any shape for company," Kieran said. "You're probably best to come by the clinic. It's easier. Not as far."

He pulled a business card out of his wallet and extended it to Jeffers, who took no notice of it. Kieran let it fall to the table.

"Vineland's not a bad drive. Just down the road. Besides, it will give me an excuse to pick up a few bottles from Tawse Winery. My wife loves the sparkling Riesling."

"The house really isn't near there."

"That's okay. Nothing's really too far from anything once you're in that neck of the woods."

Jeffers sat with his pen poised over his notebook and Kieran gave the address.

"I think that's all for now," Jeffers said, rising from his seat. "Thank you, Kieran. This has been extremely helpful. Please get in touch if you remember anything else."

Jeffers collected Kieran's card from the table and gave our host his own in return. I finished the last of my lemonade.

"God, that apartment was a sauna," Jeffers said when we were back on the street. "And it's only marginally better out here."

"You should have had the lemonade. I'm fine," I said.

"I don't buy into all that ooga booga stuff. Cilantro and lemonade. You've got to be kidding me," he said, getting into the car and cranking the air conditioner.

"It's not ooga booga. It's true what he said about cilantro having a cooling effect. I've heard that before. Why do you think they put it in spicy food?"

"To be honest, I've never given it any thought. And I'm not going to start now. I've got other things to think about."

He pulled out his phone and made a call. "Hey, it's Jeffers. I'm going to text you a phone number for a Keesha. Find out what you can. I'm also going to send you an address. See what you can dig up about the property. Oh, and run another check on Kieran Martin. Thanks."

Jeffers ended the call and proceeded to send the texts he'd mentioned.

"You think Kieran's involved?"

"I don't know. I can't get a read on that guy one way or the other. But something about him seems odd. I mean, what's a medical herbalist?"

"It's not a reason to suspect someone of murder," I said.

Jeffers veered the car into traffic.

"You know how things are nowadays," I continued. "There's a backlash against traditional medicine. A lot of people are looking for more natural alternatives. Just because you've never heard of a medical herbalist doesn't mean it's not a real thing."

"Had you ever heard of such a thing before today?"

"Not specifically but—" I was cut off by a ping from my phone. Jeffers' phone chirped a second later. We'd both received the same text.

"It's Paul," I said, reading. "He found Gray Klassen."

Chapter 13

"I was able to get a message to him through an old friend of ours," Paul said over speakerphone. "I left my number and mentioned that I had a detective friend who wanted to speak with him about Bernadelle. He texted me within the hour and said he'd be able to call tonight. We can Zoom. Does that work for you?"

"Yes," Jeffers said. "Did he mention a time?"

"He just said tonight."

"Can you ask him if nine will work? Or anytime after that? What time zone is he in?"

"He didn't say and I don't think it matters. I'll text him now and let you know what he says. How's everything going there?"

"You ever heard of such thing as a medical herbalist?" Jeffers asked.

"No."

"See, it's not a thing," Jeffers said to me. "He would know. He's a doctor."

"He's a vet," I said.

"He's still a doctor."

"Yes," I said. "But for animals."

"*He's* still on the line," Paul said. "And he's assuming that has something to do with herbal therapy. Plants and stuff."

"Yes," I said.

Jeffers looked grumpy.

"I'm not familiar with the term, that's all. In veterinary medicine we make no distinction in title. Veterinarians who want to must go through very specific training in order to be able to practice herbal medicine. They're still just called vets, though."

"You do that hippie medicine on animals?" Jeffers asked.

"I don't," Paul said. "But people do. Alternative medicine is growing in popularity among people and pets. Listen, I have to go. I have one more appointment."

"Okay, we'll see you later," I said. "You'll pick up Moustache and bring him to your place?"

"Yup."

"Oh, and if you're going by the grocery store," I said, "can you buy some cilantro?"

Jeffers shot me a look and then rolled his eyes.

"When did you become such a grouchy old man?" I asked after hanging up with Paul.

"What?"

"Ooga booga this, hippie that."

"I just like my medicine to be medicine."

My phone beeped. "We're on for nine," I said, reading the text.

"Good. But in the meantime, we've got to stay focused on Milla. Now that the initial shock has worn off, I think

I'll be able to get more from Ellen and the sister. And I don't want to mention anything about Kieran just yet."

"Why not?"

"Kieran said no one knew about their relationship. I don't want the Koeppers to get their hopes up that we've found a suspect. And I certainly don't want anyone taking matters into their own hands."

"*Is* Kieran a suspect?"

"He's not *not* a suspect."

Jeffers phone vibrated and he hit the Bluetooth button on his dashboard.

"Jeffers here."

"Hey there. I got a read off that phone number." A male voice filled the car. "It belongs to a Keesha Rodrigues."

"Is there an address for her? Did she report it stolen or missing?"

"No. But someone reported her missing."

Jeffers and I looked at each other.

"Go on," Jeffers said.

"Her mother filed a missing persons report last June. The 29th to be exact."

"I need you to send me that file. Everything you have."

"You got it," the voice said and rang off.

"Damn it!"

"The timing checks out with what Kieran said. He said Milla called him from Keesha's phone about a year ago."

Jeffers directed the Bluetooth to redial the number.

"Slatterly," said the same voice as before.

"I also want the phone records for that number," Jeffers said.

"Okay."

Jeffers hung up just as we pulled into the driveway of a ranch-style house on a tree-lined residential street. If the house had been a little further down, it surely would have had a view of the lake. Rodney Koepper stepped out onto a porch that ran most of the width of his home.

"We're set up out back," he said. "I was keeping an eye out. I hope you don't mind sitting outside. It's a beautiful evening now that the temperature is going down somewhat."

"That sounds lovely," I said.

Rodney and Jeffers shook hands.

"If it gets too warm, we can move inside," Rodney said, ushering us through the living room of the main floor.

There was a stack of bridal magazines on the coffee table. Rodney caught me noticing them.

"Sarah's getting married next spring," Rodney said. "You should have seen this place before we tidied up. Fabric samples, invitation templates, cake designs. She and Ellen have had wedding fever since Sarah announced her engagement."

Rodney was smiling as he talked. I would have bet money he was suffering a little from the affliction too.

"We're right through here. Ellen's made some snacks and some lemonade."

"It better not be green," Jeffers said under his breath and I poked him in the back.

"That's very kind," I said to Rodney. "There was no need to go to any trouble."

"No trouble at all. Please," Rodney said, sliding open a screen door and welcoming us into his backyard haven.

The garden was lush, the landscaping perfect. Ellen and Sarah were already seated on one of the outdoor couches and Rodney motioned for Jeffers and me to make ourselves comfortable on the other while he settled into a chair.

Again, Rodney's gaze pierced my soul. It was the look of someone who had suffered great loss and who could recognize it in others. A kinship of the grieving. I averted my eyes and took an avid interest in the array of garden-party hors d'oeuvres that had been set out on the table in the centre. There was also a large glass pitcher of suitably yellow lemonade that was sure to meet with Jeffers' approval.

Ellen immediately began hostessing—filling glasses, passing plates. Sarah helped but passed on taking anything for herself. Jeffers made a show of taking a large swallow of lemonade and praising Ellen, which was entirely for my benefit.

I checked the time and saw that we needed to hurry the pleasantries along and get to the point if we were going to finish up here in time to get back for Gray Klassen's phone call.

I cleared my throat and tried my best to communicate this subliminally to Jeffers, who was in the middle of a conversation with Ellen about the hydrangeas in her garden and how they never grow to that size in his own backyard.

Whether or not my telepathic powers did the trick, Jeffers quickly moved on to why we were here.

"So, you haven't found out anything new?" Sarah asked.

"Nothing we can share right now," Jeffers said. "But as I mentioned to Rodney, it would really help to get a feel for what Milla's mindset was when she left. It might help us understand where she might have gone and, from there..."

Ellen went on to echo much of what Rodney had said when we met with him over hot dogs. She and Milla had had a difficult relationship.

"No matter what I did, it was the wrong thing," Ellen said. "But I kept trying. It was all I could do."

"And what about you?" Jeffers asked Sarah.

She sighed. "I know Uncle Rod and Aunt Ellen don't like me saying this, but I feel like what happened to Milla was all my fault."

Both Rodney and Ellen interjected with words to the contrary. Ellen reached out and took Sarah's hand.

"Deep down I know it wasn't," Sarah said, silencing their protestations. "I know Milla was going through stuff and was having a hard time adjusting. I do. But I can't help but wonder if things had been a little harder for me too, then maybe she wouldn't have felt so alone and we would have adapted together. Like we'd always done."

"But it was easy for you?" I asked.

Sarah looked at her aunt and uncle and gave Ellen's hand a squeeze. "I felt like this was my home right away. Don't misunderstand, I loved my parents, but it was a hard life. And here … they just gave us so much. Not things. I don't mean that. But stability, and love, and structure, and … safety. I think that was the biggest thing. I felt safe here immediately."

"And Milla didn't?"

"Maybe she did at first. Or maybe she didn't really notice much of a difference. When we were little, I tried to shield her as best I could from what was going on. I never let her see our parents when they were at their worst. The foster homes we were sent to were fine but not great. We weren't mistreated, but we weren't loved either. Every time we moved, I made it out to be some big adventure so she wouldn't be scared.

"No matter where we were, the biggest constant in her life was me. I promised her we would never be separated. That we would always be together and that I would never let anything happen to her. The two of us against the world.

And when we came here…" Sarah's eyes started to well up. "It was just so nice to have someone take care of me," she said, shakily. "Of both of us. And I just…" She took a minute to get herself under control. "I didn't pull away from her. Not intentionally. But it wasn't just the two of us anymore. And she resented that. And she didn't trust that this was our forever home. She thought it was just another stop on our adventure and that I was being careless in allowing myself to get so close to Uncle Rod and Aunt Ellen. We fought about that a lot. And grew more and more distant."

"Did she confide in you that she was planning to leave?" Jeffers asked.

Sarah shook her head.

"And she never came by again? In all this time?"

"No," said Ellen. "We looked for her. Rodney was out every day. I checked in with the school regularly, but she never went in. Eventually, I started going to shelters with her picture telling the people there to let her know if they ever saw her that she was welcome to come home when she was ready and that we loved her. Whether she ever got the message, I have no idea."

As Ellen talked, I noticed Sarah shift uncomfortably in her chair. When I managed to catch her eye, she quickly looked away.

"May I use your washroom?" I asked, interrupting Ellen's narrative.

"Of course," Rodney said, rising. "It's—"

"Sarah, would you mind showing me the way?"

Sarah smiled graciously and led me into the house. When we were safely out of view and earshot, I turned on her.

"Milla came by here, didn't she?" I said.

"No, I haven't—"

"Sarah, I was watching you while Ellen was talking. It's obvious you know something. Something you don't want your aunt and uncle to know. And that's fine. I promise not to tell them, but I need you to tell me."

I don't know how I was so sure, but there was no doubt in my mind that Milla had come by the house, just as she'd planned.

"You're wrong. She didn't—"

"April 17th. Four years ago."

Sarah's mouth fell open. "How do you know that?"

"It doesn't matter how I know. What matters is that you do. And I need you to tell me everything."

Chapter 14

Sarah pulled me into the powder room and shut the door.

"All right, yes," she said. "Milla came by. No one else was here but me."

"And you haven't told your aunt and uncle?"

Sarah shook her head. "I couldn't."

"What do you mean?"

"I couldn't do that to them. Not after everything they'd done to find her. After everything they'd gone through. They had finally come to terms with Milla being gone, and I just couldn't let them see her like that."

"Like what? Happy?"

"What? No! Who told you that?"

"I can't say," I said.

And at that moment, I really couldn't. I could barely think. Sarah's revelation had knocked me off my feet.

"Well, whoever said that was lying. Milla showed up here out of nowhere, stoned out of her mind on god knows what and in a panic about some guy who wouldn't leave her alone. She was terrified. She begged me to help her get away from him."

"What did you do?"

"She refused to come in. Said she wanted nothing to do with Ellen and Rod. She told me she'd been watching the house, waiting for them to leave. And, given the state she was in, I was just as happy they hadn't seen her. It would have destroyed them. Uncle Rod especially. So, I took her to my boyfriend's place and made sure she ate something and slept off the high. The next day, she asked me to call the guy who'd been hassling her and pretend to be her. I told him I never wanted to see him again, that everything had been a mistake, and to stop calling me. Then I blocked his number."

"What happened after that?"

"She stayed for a couple of days. She said she needed help getting off the drugs and wanted to get clean. I promised to help but she took off a few days later."

"And you never saw her again?"

"No."

"Do you remember the name of the man she was running from?"

"On her phone, he just came up as 'K.'"

I took a deep breath, not knowing what to make of what Sarah had just told me. "Okay," I said. "Thank you."

"Please don't tell my aunt and uncle. They wouldn't understand why I kept it from them."

"I'm not sure I do either," I said.

"Milla had been missing for two years, and it nearly destroyed us. We all blamed ourselves. Punished ourselves. Every moment was filled with thoughts of Milla. We were ... shadows of the people we'd once been. But we had started to get back to where we were. We had started connecting again. Living again. And then Milla showed up, still so full of hostility toward them and I…

"If she had stayed and gotten clean, I would have brought her back here. I would have told them. I wanted to. But she was filled with so much hate. And she was gone again before I could even think what to do next." She paused, her eyes appealing to me. "All they wanted to do was love her. It would have broken their hearts."

I considered this and honestly didn't know if it would be better for Ellen and Rodney to know or not. At this point, I wasn't sure it would even make a difference.

"I have to tell my partner what you've told me," I said.

She nodded. I could see she was on the verge of tears.

"And Sarah, if there is anything else, *anything*, you need to tell me right now."

"There's not. I promise." Tears started to stream down her cheeks. "I'm sorry," she said. "I know I should have said something earlier, but I just didn't know how."

"Come here," I said, taking her into my arms as she collapsed into sobs. "You told us now. You did the right thing."

"Do you think that guy had something to do with it?"

"I don't know," I said gently.

What I did know was that if Kieran wasn't a suspect before, he was now.

Jeffers slammed his hand against the steering wheel. I didn't know if it was in reaction to what I had just told him about my conversation with Sarah or the fact that we were stuck waiting for a bridge to lower and were going to be late for our 9:00 p.m. phone call with Gray Klassen. Maybe a combination of the two.

The Niagara Peninsula is traversed by the Welland Canal, which connects Lake Ontario and Lake Erie and enables ships—commercial and otherwise—to negotiate the Niagara Escarpment and avoid Niagara Falls. There is a series of locks that raise and lower the water level as needed and they are all outfitted with movable bridges that raise as the boats pass.

I was sure the canal system had given birth to some of the more colourful curse words as you can almost always guarantee that, if you're running late, the bridge will invariably be up at the desired crossing. On the flip side, you can always create fictional bridge disruptions to your advantage. It was possible to race to the next bridge over to catch it as it came down or before it went up, but that was always a crapshoot. The worst was when you arrived at the bridge just as the crossing arms were being lowered—you knew you were in for a long wait. Fortunately, when Jeffers and I joined the line of waiting cars, the boat was partway through.

"I knew there was something off about that guy," Jeffers said, turning off the car.

"We don't know he had anything to do with it. Sarah said she blocked his number and—"

"Numbers can be unblocked."

"Yes, but—"

"And Sarah also said Milla took off again. She could very easily have gone back to him or, at least, got back in touch. And then who knows what. You saw the guy. Not exactly a chick magnet. If he thought his only girlfriend was trying to leave him, maybe he did whatever he could to make sure that didn't happen."

"*But*," I said emphatically, hoping Jeffers wouldn't interrupt me again, "it's not just Milla's death we're investigating. Angela Hansen. Bernadelle Klassen. Who knows how many others?"

Jeffers sighed. "Keesha Rodrigues."

"Keesha might still be alive," I said.

"I hope so. And I'd like to keep it that way."

"The other cases date back ten years. At least. Kieran would have only been nineteen or twenty."

"There have been killers a lot younger than that," Jeffers said.

"I know that. He just doesn't strike me as a criminal mastermind."

"I'm not saying he's the ringleader," Jeffers said. "But he could very definitely be involved."

We took a moment, silently agreeing to disagree.

"I gave Sarah my number," I said when the dust had settled. "I told her to call if she remembers anything else or if she just needs to talk."

"That's good. It's clear she trusts you."

"It's been four years since it happened. It's not exactly fresh in her mind but maybe our conversation will dredge something up. Something she thought was insignificant at the time."

"And maybe Gray Klassen will fill in a few blanks too."

Jeffers and I walked in on Paul and Gray sharing a laugh as they reminisced about the antics of one of their former classmates. Paul shot me a relieved look when we appeared in the living room. I guessed both men had just about exhausted their arsenals of small talk.

Moustache ran out from the kitchen, tail wagging madly, and jumped up, wiggling in enjoyment as I scratched and nuzzled him.

Jeffers quickly moved in front of Paul's computer screen, introduced himself, and apologized for our lateness.

"Bridge," I said quietly to Paul and he rolled his eyes in understanding.

We joined Jeffers on the couch.

Moustache tried to worm his way between us, but as were all sitting so close together in order to properly see the screen and be seen by the camera, he settled for putting his head on my knee and nosing my hand whenever it stopped petting him.

There was a plain, white sheet hanging behind Gray that effectively covered any distinguishable features and, therefore, anything that might give a clue to his whereabouts. There was also a soundlessness about the room. No ambient noise, no outside traffic or rustle of wind. Not a chirp or a bark. It was a little eerie. There was probably something much more high-tech and out of the realm of my imagination at play as well that was ensuring his security but, in good CSIS form, it was appropriately invisible.

"So, Paul said this has something to do with Bernadelle," Gray said. "I'm assuming you've caught someone."

"Not quite," Jeffers said and went on to briefly explain how he believed Bernadelle's death was connected to a string of other suspicious and similar deaths.

Gray looked crestfallen at the news that his sister's killer remained at large. It had been a long time with no closure, and I could see he had gotten his hopes up.

"I'm sorry we don't have anything more concrete at this time," Jeffers said, obviously picking up on the same disappointment I was.

Gray nodded and shook it off. "So, what do you need from me?" he asked.

"I don't even know," Jeffers admitted, pulling out his notebook. "We're just trying to understand more of what Bernadelle's mindset might have been at the time. Get to know her better. Something might trigger a parallel with one of the other cases."

"Well, she was going through a hard time but was good at putting on a brave face."

"We know she and her boyfriend had recently broken up. Is there any chance he could have—"

"Mirsad? No way. He was truly the salt of the earth. The best guy. He had nothing to do with her disappearance. Besides, he wasn't even in the province."

"Okay."

"The break-up was devastating for both of them. I know he took it particularly hard. It was a surprise to him. To all of us. Came out of the blue, really."

"So, she was the one who ended things?"

Gray nodded.

"Do you know why?"

Gray sighed. His face remained unexpressive, but his body language told me he was struggling with how to answer. There was something lingering that he wasn't sure he should share, I could tell.

"Mr. Klassen, was Bernadelle pregnant when she went missing?" I asked.

"What makes you think that?" he said.

"Was she?" Jeffers asked. Gray remained silent. "Look, we want to find out who is responsible for your sister's death and we need your help. You need to tell us everything you know."

"Even if means breaking a confidence," I added.

There was a long pause then Gray said, "She hadn't told my parents. She knew they would disapprove. And she hadn't said anything about it to Mirsad. As far as I know, I was the only one she told and when she disappeared, I … I didn't want to add to my parents' grief."

"Is that why she ended the relationship?" I asked.

"Mirsad had just landed an amazing opportunity in Alberta and was being groomed for great things. Bernadelle knew he would drop everything for her and the baby, and she didn't want that."

"Would he have had to?" I asked. "I mean, couldn't he have kept his job and had a family?"

Gray shrugged. "Probably. If Bernadelle moved out there. But she wouldn't. She seemed to think it was all too complicated. And too soon. She said Mirsad had worked so hard to get where he was and she wanted him to be able to enjoy it. She didn't want to jeopardize it in any way. And she didn't want to put him in a position where he felt he had to choose. It was all just bad timing."

"So, what reason did she give him?"

"At the time my father was having some heart trouble. She made it sound worse than it was and said she didn't want to be away from the family while he was sick. Even if he got better, his condition made her realize she would never be comfortable being so far away from home."

"Did she ever think of terminating the pregnancy?" Jeffers asked.

"No," Gray said. "Well, that's not entirely true. I know she did think about it but could never bring herself to do it. However, she also knew once our parents found out she was expecting, they would probably tell Mirsad or his parents, which was the very thing she wanted to avoid. The whole situation was really starting to cause her a lot of stress."

"What about adoption?" I asked.

"I really don't know what she was going to do. I don't think she knew. She was pretty much going day to day and trying to fill her time with as much as possible to avoid thinking about it. And to avoid being around our parents. She was working whenever she could. Always picking up extra shifts—at the store or at the centre where she volunteered."

"And where was that?" Jeffers asked.

"The Salvation Army. She helped out in the food bank a few days a week. They used to be down on Gilmore Road. My guess is they're still there."

"Was it possible Bernadelle left town voluntarily?"

"I did wonder about that," Gray said. "I mean, she knew she couldn't hide the pregnancy forever. So, yeah, I guess it's definitely possible. But whether she did or didn't, it doesn't change the fact that someone killed her."

"No, it doesn't," I said.

"Do you know a Kieran Martin, by any chance?" Jeffers asked.

"No," Gray said without any hesitation.

"He would have been younger than Bernadelle by a few years. A bit nerdy. Into science," Jeffers said, hoping one of the descriptions might jog Gray's memory.

"Sorry," Gray said, shaking his head. "Does he have something to with this?"

"We're not sure. I'd appreciate you not mentioning his name to anyone until we know more."

"Of course."

"Okay," Jeffers said, closing his notebook. "This is good."

"You get anything that might help?" Gray asked.

"We sure did," Jeffers said.

Gray, working for whom he worked for, knew better than to ask for details.

Jeffers left Gray with some words of reassurance that everything was being done to find the people responsible for his sister's death and promised to be in touch again once we knew more.

Paul took over signing-off duties and Jeffers and I moved into the kitchen, followed by Moustache, who went straight to his dish in the hope of finding something new.

A breeze blew the cat door open and Moustache vanished from the room so fast his paws barely touched the ground.

Jeffers smiled.

"He probably thought Brimstone was making an appearance," I said.

"That's not what I'm smiling about," he said.

"All right, Sherlock, what's got you all chuffed?"

"We have a lead, Samuel. A real, bona fide lead."

"Bernadelle being pregnant? I know. I just about squealed when Gray mentioned that. I mean it's—"

"Not the pregnancy. Although I admit, yes, that really solidifies things. Good call on that by the way. But think about what else Gray said. About how Bernadelle kept busy…"

"Work, the food bank," I said.

"The food bank. Bernadelle volunteered at one and—"

"Angela Hansen was last seen at a soup kitchen," I finished for him. "Oh!"

"Yup. I gotta go," he said, turning to leave. "Call me tomorrow after you meet with the adoption people."

Paul was on his hands and knees with his head inside the hall closet, and Jeffers nearly tripped over him on his way out.

"What are you doing?" I asked.

"I'm trying to talk Moustache into coming out," he said, his voice muffled by the closet's contents.

I knelt down next to him and stuck my head inside. Moustache was perched on top of various pairs of shoes and boots and had pressed himself up against the far wall, the top of his head obscured by coats. He was shaking.

"Moo, the cat's not here," I said as gently as possible. "Why don't you come out?"

Paul and I looked at each other. "I'm going in," I said.

I cleared a small path and crawled to the dog. He side-eyed me, probably afraid a bigger movement might disclose his whereabouts to the enemy.

I soothed and stroked and snuggled and eventually he relaxed into me and licked my face.

Paul stuck his head back in, waggling a glass of wine at me and a bully stick at Moustache. The dog's ears twitched and he cocked his head, sniffing the air. A moment later he bounded out of the closet and was happily chewing in the living room by the time I clumsily emerged on my hands and knees.

The bag of wedding rings fell out of my pocket. I grabbed it then held out my hand, hoping Paul would help me up.

"Um…" he said. "Are you…?"

I looked at myself on my knees holding a bag of rings and quickly and gracelessly scrambled to my feet.

"I am not proposing," I stammered, suddenly acutely aware and incredibly self-conscious. "These are from Jeffers."

"Oh. Jeffers is proposing."

"Jeffers thinks it would be better if we were 'married,'" I said and went on to explain the rationale.

"Cool," he said, taking the bag and handing me the glass of wine in return.

We plopped ourselves down on the living room couch and Paul proceeded to try on rings while I watched and took bigger than usual sips from my glass.

"Your turn," he said, sliding the bag to me once he had chosen.

"Did you really think I was proposing?" I asked.

"No. I was kidding. Although I did find the presentation of twenty different rings an interesting choice. I'll have to keep that in mind," he said, giving me a wink and disappearing into the kitchen.

My heart and my stomach fluttered simultaneously and I grabbed one of the rings and jammed it onto my finger.

It felt odd but strangely comfortable at the same time. It wasn't really my style. Although I had to admit, until that moment, I hadn't given much thought as to what "my style" might be for something like this.

And I wasn't sure I wanted to.

I shook the thought out of my head and reminded myself the ring was only there for the benefit of the nice adoption practitioner/baby trafficker.

Just another costume.

So why was it making my insides dance?

Chapter 15

"I feel sick to my stomach."

"Let it go, Bells," Paul said. "It didn't bother me."

"Well, it should have. She was rude, arrogant, judgmental. She didn't even bother to hear the context. She acted like you were a serial killer."

"Well, at least we know *she* isn't one. Or in cahoots with one."

I was fuming after the meeting with the first adoption practitioner. She had mounted her high horse as soon as Paul's criminal record was mentioned and proceeded to peer down on us, condemnation seeping from every pore, sweeping the possibility of adoption off the table with one mighty swing of her self-righteous arm.

"How are you not mad about this?" I asked.

"Because that woman in there doesn't know a single thing about me. She looks at me and sees me in a black-and-white striped jumpsuit with a ball and chain hanging off my ankle. And that's it. I know the kind of man I am.

Besides, in all honesty, it sounded to me like she was more horrified to discover you were an actress than I was a criminal."

I giggled as I recalled the woman's look of disdain as she recorded my occupation on her precious intake form.

"Yes, she's probably of the very Victorian opinion that actresses and prostitutes are one and the same."

"She probably holds a very Victorian opinion about a lot of things," Paul said, adding his laughter to mine.

"She can't be too prim though," I said. "This place is on a list of organizations the police have been looking at for a while. She may not be a part of the baby ring, but there's got to be something going on there for the police to have taken notice."

A text from Jeffers appeared on my phone. *Text me when you're done.*

We're done.

My phone rang almost immediately.

"How'd it go?"

"She's not part of it. She practically gave us the Sermon on the Mount," I said then filled Jeffers in on the highlights.

"Okay. When's your next meeting?"

"In about an hour. We're going to head over shortly. How are things there? Anything on Keesha Rodrigues?"

I heard the rustle of papers.

"Twenty-eight years old. Her mother reported her missing when she didn't come home from work. She was a manager at Zees."

"In Niagara-on-the-Lake?"

"The very one."

"She lived with her mother?"

"She did but…"

"But what?" Silence. "Jeffers?"

"Keesha had moved back in with her mom about two months earlier. She'd been raped and was afraid to be living alone. She had only just returned to work."

"And?" I asked, even though I knew what was coming.

"She'd just found out she was pregnant."

"So that's four women. That we know of."

"Yeah. I'm going to head over and talk to her mother right now. Lindsey and Crayne are working the food bank angle. We've got people digging into everything we can think of. The dark web is turning out to be a dead end, but we'll keep monitoring activity though as it's likely something might pop up if your next visit turns out to be promising."

"You'll be the first to know."

"Dr. and Mrs. Barrett," the second adoption practitioner began.

Paul and I had introduced ourselves to the stuffy, middle-aged, tweed-wearing man behind the desk and completed the initial paperwork, where we listed my address as "ours" but used our individual surnames. Arnold Reymer, as we came to know him, was quick to confide that he had seen me onstage at the Shaw the previous year but had never tuned in to *Port Authority* when it had been on, insinuating that it had been far beneath his intellectual prowess. I imagined his idea of chilling out in front of the TV was watching an episode of *Masterpiece Theatre* or a documentary narrated by Sir Richard Attenborough.

Regardless of his superior artistic tastes, his admission enabled me to play the celebrity card and express my desire for his utmost discretion, laying on thick that this was a highly personal matter, one I was not eager to share with the press.

He had given me an all-knowing nod, patted my hand in reassurance, and from that moment on began using the formal, matrimonial address when speaking to us. I guessed he was the type who would also favour the very traditional "Mrs. Paul Barrett" and I could picture him seated at a writing table, dressed in a velvet smoking jacket, dipping a fountain pen in ink, and artfully writing the name on a place card.

In his mind, the title was his way of giving me my desired privacy, so I had no choice but to embrace my Barrettness for the remainder of the meeting.

"I am afraid Dr. Barrett's criminal record has created a bit of a pickle for us," he said, obviously enjoying his use of the word "pickle" and how witty he believed it made him seem.

The man had been pleasant enough at the start. He had welcomed us warmly, kindly offered the usual refreshments, and made some effort to get to know us before praising the nobility of adoption and the beauty of family. All of which, however, he carried off with the dullest of expressions and the most monotone of voices.

His whole demeanour changed when the criminal record had been introduced. He sat up straighter, the corners of his mouth bent ever so slightly upward, and his voice took on a crispness that had been absent up to that point.

"You see," he said, addressing Paul, "you're not eligible for a pardon for a few more years and, once you begin the appeal, that process can take some time. I can't even begin the particulars of your adoption application until the pardon is granted. Then, provided all the paperwork passes, I'll have to schedule a home study, which typically takes two to three months. Once you are cleared as prospective parents—if you're cleared—we will enter the matching phase. Some couples match very quickly while others have a harder time. After you're matched, you'll have to wait out the duration of the pregnancy. And then there is the finalization period, which consists of several post-placement visits over a six-month period. All in all, in your case, I don't anticipate you adopting for about five years. Minimum."

"Five years?" Paul and I said together.

"As I said, it could be longer. And there are no guarantees, even with the pardon, that your application will be accepted." He had coloured the details of the lengthy process with thick commiseration and delivered this last statement with direst sympathy.

Paul and I both put on our most devastated faces. The more hopeless the situation, the more likely an alternative might be presented. It was exactly what we wanted. Strangely, I got the feeling it was what Arnold Reymer wanted too.

"Dr. and Mrs. Barrett, I am so sorry. You seem like lovely people and I'm sure you would have made wonderful parents—"

"Would have made?" I said. "You make it sound like there's no chance for us. I realize five years is a long time, but that doesn't mean it's hopeless."

"Mrs. Barrett…"

"Is it? Hopeless?"

My eyes filled with tears. One of the gifts some actors possess—the ability to cry on cue. I had a lot of loss to tap into and years of unshed tears just waiting to fall. Paul reached out and took my hand.

My crying seemed to stoke whatever fire had ignited within Arnold when the criminal record was disclosed. If there had been an ounce of sexuality in him, I would have said that he seemed a little aroused by the predicament.

He didn't answer my question but rather adopted an expression that suggested we had surpassed the limits of possibility long ago.

"There must be something we can do," I said, appealing to Paul, who seemed a little surprised himself by my emotions. "This is our dream. We're meant to have a family. I can't have children. This is our only way. There's got to be—"

I was laying it on thick and, thankfully, Paul followed my lead perfectly.

"Shhh, it's all right, honey," Paul said, bringing my hand to his lips and kissing it gently. "I promised you this record wouldn't get in the way of our having a child and I meant it. We'll try somewhere else. And somewhere else after that if need be. We'll do whatever it takes." Paul rose from his seat.

I responded with a dejected nod and happened to catch Arnold disguising a smile as a cough.

"Mr. Reymer, thank you very much for your time. You have been most forthcoming," I said, pushing my chair back and making to stand.

He was on his feet before I could lift my backside off the chair's cushion.

"Dr. and Mrs. Barrett, if you please," he said, motioning for us to resume our seats.

My instinct had been right. I was positive stodgy Arnold had his hand in something. If we played things carefully, we could get what we needed to dismantle the whole baby ring and find out what happened to Milla.

Paul and I looked at each other, and I fought the urge to let the excitement that was coursing through my veins show on my face. Paul gave my hand a squeeze as we sat, and I knew he was feeling the same.

"I sympathize with what you're going through. I really do," Arnold said. "But no matter where you go, all prospective adoption applicants are required, by law, to undergo an extensive background check. I'm very sorry, but the only way you will ever be allowed to move beyond the initial stages of the application process is if—"

"I'm pardoned, yes, you said that," Paul said.

"That's right," said Arnold, looking intently from Paul to me. "Of course, if your record didn't exist at all…"

"What are you saying?" I asked.

"I'm saying that things would be easier and faster for you both if Dr. Barrett's criminal record was … expunged."

I sat up a little straighter in my chair. "But that's impossible," I said.

"Mrs. Barrett, nothing is impossible," Arnold said. "If you want it badly enough."

Chapter 16

"And just how much would this expungement cost?" Jeffers asked.

"A hundred thousand," Paul said.

Paul and I were heading home and had Jeffers on speakerphone.

"My god," Jeffers said. "So that's his game. He's offering to alter records so applications appear clean."

"I'm not sure 'offering' is the right word," I said.

"And I'll bet you every cent of that money it doesn't stop at criminal records. Health histories, financials…"

"Who knows how many babies he's helped to place in precarious homes," I said.

"This is good work," Jeffers said. "Lindsey's going to love this."

Paul and I gave each other silent congratulations.

"How did you leave things with Arnold?"

"We told him we'd like some time to consider it and that we'd have to look over our finances, of course."

"And Bella positively gushed with gratitude," Paul added.

"Perfect. He needs to think he's sitting pretty," Jeffers said.

"I also peppered in some doubt," I said. "Played the celebrity card like you wanted and ramped up my anxiety about what it might do to my career if things ever got out, blah, blah, blah, dropped in a 'maybe we shouldn't'…"

"As soon as she said that, he pretty much fell all over himself with assurances of confidentiality and discretion," Paul said with a laugh.

"Excellent. Okay, you're going to wait a couple of days before getting in touch with him again. That will give Lindsey and her team time to coordinate a plan and Arnold a chance to make contact with his people. With any luck, we might finally see some action on the dark web. Either Lindsey or I will tell you how to proceed. She may want to stretch this out. We're going to need some irrefutable proof before we can go in there and shut him down."

"I recorded the whole thing on my phone," I said. "Will that do?"

"It's a good start, but it's not enough. He's very likely not involved with whoever killed Milla and the others," Lindsey said.

Paul had done a small detour to drop me at the station before heading back to the clinic. After I told Jeffers I'd recorded the conversation with Arnold Reymer, he wanted to hear it right away. Lindsey, Steven, and Staff Sergeant Crayne were all waiting with Jeffers when I arrived.

"You don't think?" Jeffers asked.

"Like we said when Ms. James joined us, the people we're dealing with would use Dr. Barrett's criminal record to their advantage," Lindsey said. "They'd say his record is an obstacle standing in their way of becoming parents. They would offer an alternative to traditional adoption rather than offer to get rid of the obstacle. Obstacles are what they're counting on. They need them for their business to succeed."

"So Arnold Reymer is running a completely different racket?"

"It would seem so," Crayne said.

"Maybe not completely," Steven's voice rang out from behind a monitor. "I'm looking over his financials … um … his off-shore accounts," he clarified for my benefit in case I didn't understand the word. "There are deposits of a hundred thousand dollars dating back years but—"

"Yes, we know about those," said Lindsey before Steven could finish. "They're why he's been on our radar. And now, it's pretty safe to say, we know what they're from."

"But what about the transactions for twenty-five thousand dollars?"

"Those occur shortly after a one-hundred-thousand-dollar payment," Lindsey explained to Jeffers and me. None of what Steven said was new information for Lindsey and Crayne. "There's a twenty-five-thousand-dollar withdrawal a couple of days after each deposit. He's obviously working with someone who is doing the actual altering of records and compensating them."

"I'm not talking about those," Steven said. "I'm talking about twenty-five-thousand-dollar deposits."

He turned the computer screen toward us so we could all see the five transactions he had highlighted.

Jeffers and I looked to Lindsey and Crayne who, in turn, looked at each other.

"There are five such deposits over a nine-year period. The last one was only a few months ago."

"Is there a withdrawal after those as well?" Crayne asked.

"Nope."

"My guess would be he's providing two different services," Crayne said.

"One that's clearly more lucrative than the other," said Steven.

"Which may be why there are so few of those transactions," Lindsey said.

"Okay, let me get this straight," Jeffers said, drawing our attention away from the screen. "You're thinking Arnold's *first* move is to convince people to have their records altered. He stands to make seventy-five thousand dollars every time someone agrees, so it's in his best interest to offer this as option A. If they refuse, he presents option B. He doesn't stand to make nearly as much money, but he's still coming out twenty-five-thousand-dollars in the black."

"And you think option B could be buying a baby?" I asked. "That doesn't seem like nearly enough money."

Jeffers looked to Crayne and Lindsey for an answer.

"It's not. But it might be the price of a referral," Crayne said. "These transactions could definitely place him inside the ring. This is good work. Lindsey, get your people on this. Comb through all the transactions of the people who have been flagged. See if there's anything similar. And check them against the dates of the missing women. We know they had multiple births and it will be near impossible to know exactly when the babies were born but, if we're lucky, there might be a pattern, and if we're really lucky, it might give us an idea as to how many women are involved." Lindsey nodded. "Jeffers, I want you and Bella to come with me to see Morris. We need to figure out a game plan for your next meeting with Mr. Reymer. We've got to play this carefully. We don't know for certain he's part of the bigger picture, and we don't want to risk losing what we already have on him. One wrong move could blow the whole thing up."

Chapter 17

"We're going to refuse to have my record erased?" Paul asked.

"Yes," Jeffers said. "Only after expressing a lot of regret and second-guessing. We need him to think he can still get something out of you."

"Even if it's only twenty-five thousand dollars," I said.

Jeffers had driven me home after our meeting with Morris and was filling Paul in on the plan.

Moustache listened from where he was splayed out on the kitchen floor, cooling his belly. This was normally the time we'd be out for a walk, but the afternoons of late were much too hot for him. We had altered our routine to include a long walk early in the morning and a short jaunt around the neighbourhood before bed.

"And you can't get too moralistic with your decision to refuse," Jeffers went on. "We want him to think he still has a chance you'll accept another shady alternative."

"What should we say?" Paul asked.

Jeffers rattled off what Crayne and Morris had come up with. We were to focus on how there were no certainties we'd be matched even with the criminal record out of the picture and play up our fear of the birth mother reneging even if we were matched. The risk of losing all that money on something that isn't a sure thing. We could also use the time consideration as an issue. The process could still take years.

"This, fingers crossed, should bring Arnold Reymer to offer door number two, which comes with more of a guarantee," I said.

"And we'll accept?" Paul asked.

"Yes," Jeffers said. "But not right away. At a third meeting. Again, we want to see if he reaches out to any of his colleagues about having a possible buyer."

"Okay. Sounds good," Paul said.

"And Bella, you'll record the meeting again."

I nodded.

"Is that even legal?" Paul asked.

"One-party consent," I said. "As long as one person involved in the conversation knows it's being recorded, they are not legally required to inform the other people taking part."

Paul looked to Jeffers for confirmation.

Jeffers nodded. "But Morris is getting us a warrant anyway. Just in case."

"So, when do we do this?" Paul asked.

"You'll call Arnold tomorrow," Jeffers said. "Tell him you've considered the arrangement and would like to meet. Refuse whatever time he offers first and accept the second. My guess is he'll want to see you again sooner rather than later."

"The sooner the better, as far as I'm concerned," I said. "I want to bring these guys down so bad I can taste it."

"We still don't know if Arnold is involved. And we still have other leads to follow," Jeffers said. "Speaking of which, I'm going to pop into Zees. See if I can learn anything more about the night Keesha Rodrigues disappeared. The staff were all interviewed at the time, but I'd like to hear from them myself."

"Do you mind if I join you?" I asked.

Zees was just a few blocks away from the Royal George Theatre and I had plenty of time to accompany Jeffers before I had to get ready for my evening performance.

"As if you have to ask."

During the brief drive downtown, Jeffers told me about his meeting with Keesha's mother. She'd told him that Keesha had called her after work on June 28th to say she had an appointment and wouldn't be home until later that evening. The mother had met some friends for dinner and assumed Keesha was in bed when she got home. The next morning, there was no sign of her daughter and she realized that Keesha had not come home the night before.

"And she didn't mention Keesha calling her again?" I asked.

"No. Why?"

"Just seems odd that if Keesha managed to keep her phone, she'd let Milla use it to call Kieran but she didn't call her own mother. Or the police. And how did Milla get Kieran's number anyway? He said she called him at the clinic, but he didn't even work there when they were together. How did Milla know about it?"

"I wish I had answers for you."

"Is it possible Keesha knew Kieran?"

"Not based on what he said," Jeffers said.

"Can we trust what he said? According to him, he and Milla were very much in love, but Sarah told me a different story."

"Hopefully her phone records have a story to tell too."

"Did Keesha's mom say anything about the rape?" I asked.

According to Mrs. Rodrigues, Keesha had been a victim of a date rape in her own apartment a few months before she went missing. She thought she'd be able to keep living there, but as time went on it became increasingly more difficult and she decided to move home. Keesha had pressed charges and an investigation was underway.

"The whole thing went up in smoke, though, when Keesha went missing," Jeffers said.

"Convenient for the guy."

"Yeah."

"Any chance he's involved in her disappearance?"

"No. He checks out."

"And what about the pregnancy?" I asked.

"According to her mother, Keesha had just found out a few days before. She was devastated."

"I can't even begin to imagine. Surviving a rape is hard enough. Adding a pregnancy…"

"Whoever's responsible for her disappearance may have offered her a quick and easy way to deal with it," Jeffers said, pulling the car to a stop in front of the restaurant.

"Maybe that was the appointment she told her mother about."

We got out of the car and walked through the gate in the white picket fence that surrounded the property, passing by the patio, which was already full of pre-theatre diners, as was the covered, wraparound porch. The inside of the restaurant was no less busy. The air held a mix of garlic and Mediterranean spices. We certainly hadn't picked a great time to come asking questions.

A waiter directed us to the manager, a man named Ross. Irritation showed on his face when Jeffers showed his badge and explained the reason for our visit, but he didn't dare express it vocally.

"Thank you for seeing us," I said as we followed Ross along a narrow hallway to an office in the back. "I know you're in the middle of the dinner rush. We'll try not to be too long."

"I'm not sure I can help," Ross said once we'd crowded ourselves into a tiny office clearly meant for one person.

Ross squeezed behind a desk that was much too large for the space. Jeffers and I stood facing him.

"You said this is about Keesha?"

"Yes," Jeffers said.

"I don't suppose…"

"No. I'm sorry—we haven't located her."

The concern on Ross' face was genuine.

"But we have come upon some new information and we're hoping it'll lead somewhere," Jeffers continued.

Ross nodded.

"In the file, it says you'd been working the last time Keesha was seen."

"Yes," Ross said. "We were both managers. She usually worked the day shift and I took the evenings."

"What can you remember from that particular day? How did Keesha seem?"

"A couple of the staff said Keesha seemed a little … distracted, but otherwise it was like any other day. She'd been through some stuff so I didn't think anything of it. She had only recently come back to work after … you know…"

"We do," I said.

"We were all just trying to keep things normal for her."

"Do you have any idea what might have been on her mind?" I asked.

I was wondering how close Keesha and Ross might have been. Whether she might have confided in him about her condition.

"Look, Keesha was a great manager. She'd been here for years. She trained me. She loved this place. But I think she may have come back to work too soon. I think she was still haunted by what happened."

I nodded my understanding and Jeffers changed the subject.

"So, how did it work?" Jeffers asked. "She worked the lunch crowd then you came on?"

"Yeah. Pretty much. Pretty simple. If something happened during the day that I needed to know about, she'd fill me in. We'd go over the evening's reservations. Stuff like that. We always had a quick changeover chat."

"And did you have one of those chats that day?"

"Yeah," Ross said, the tiniest bit of impatience colouring his response. He glanced at the door.

"We won't be much longer," I said, hoping to assuage some of his worry about being off the floor.

He smiled.

Jeffers opened his mouth to ask another question but was interrupted by Ross.

"Actually, wait. No. When I got here, Keesha was in the kitchen dealing with the Molly's Garden donation. They usually come earlier in the afternoon, but they were late that day, I remember."

"Molly's Garden?"

"It's a soup kitchen in Niagara Falls. We provide food once a week."

I let out an involuntary gasp. Jeffers caught my eye as he pulled out his notebook. I coughed to cover my reaction.

"And after that?" Jeffers asked.

"Things were starting to pick up. I was running around. Keesha gave me a brief rundown on the day and then left."

"She left alone?"

"Yes."

"Is there anything you can tell us about the person who was here from Molly's Garden?" Jeffers asked.

"I didn't see them.'

"Did the same person always pick up the food?" I asked.

"I really don't know. They usually come before I get here. Look, I'm really sorry, but I do need to get back out there."

"Of course," Jeffers said. "Thank you."

Ross led us out the way we came. The restaurant had filled considerably in the time we'd been there, and Ross was immediately swept up in requests by staff for bill adjustments and dealing with reservation snafus. I heard a small crash somewhere behind the bar.

We saw ourselves out.

"Another food bank," I said as we dodged tourists meandering down the busy main drag, hands holding shopping bags, cameras, ice cream cones.

"Yup," Jeffers said.

"Can't be a coincidence."

"Nope."

He had his phone out and was thumbing a message to someone. My guess was either Lindsey or Crayne. Or Morris.

"What do you have on tomorrow?" he asked.

"I'm off."

"Good. I want to head over to Molly's Garden and see what we can find out. I also want to pay a visit to Kieran's house in Vineland. Some paperwork about it came in earlier. I'm going to head back to the station to go over it. Do you want a ride to the theatre?"

"No," I said. "It's just down the street and the walk will help me clear my head. I need to get into the right mindset for tonight."

As I quick-stepped my way through the throng of people crowding the sidewalks, I tried to shift my own thinking into that of my character, Phoebe, but more and more her obsession with lost youth drew me back to the lost youths of the four women we knew about and those of how many more women we had yet to discover.

I arrived at the stage door, breathed in some rompishly Napoleonic merriment, and vowed to put all thoughts of missing women and babies out of my mind for the next several hours.

The universe, however, had other ideas.

Chapter 18

Strewn on the floor of my dressing room were instruments of torment. Faces of smiling babies looked up at me from pamphlets, brochures, and booklets.

"I'm so sorry. We're almost finished," Margo Livingston said from the floor where she and Adam were sitting on her yoga mat surrounded by a sea of paper.

"That's okay," I lied. "What's all this?"

"Margo's extolling the virtues of surrogacy. Word got out at the bar the other night that Powell and I were looking to adopt and Andy mentioned he and Margo had Nora via a surrogate—"

"And I was so excited when Andy came home and told me. I gathered up all the research we'd done before Nora was born and texted Adam to meet me—"

"I've been sitting on this mat for two hours. This pose is the closest I've come to doing yoga in my whole life."

I wasn't at all surprised to hear Adam's adoption plan was no longer a secret. Adam could never contain his excitement for long.

Andy Rieser was one of the lighting operators at the Festival and a regular fixture around the table when post-show drinks were being had over at the Olde Angel Inn. He was also Margo's husband.

"I'm afraid I haven't been able to convince him though," Margo said, as she got to her feet.

"Surrogacy didn't even cross our minds," Adam said, gathering the brochures into a neat pile. "But with Margo's input here, it's certainly something we'll think about. I mean, Powell's got great genes, and then we can actually choose the mother. It's like getting a designer baby!"

Margo and I looked at each other and rolled our eyes.

"I'm kidding," Adam said. "Kind of. Now one of you help me up. There's no way I'm getting up off this floor on my own."

I reached out a hand and Adam pulled himself upright.

"Hmmm," he said, taking my face in one of his hands, "you've got great cheekbones. And your—"

"Don't even think about it," I said, ushering him to the door.

"You're a little short but Powell's height might—"

I closed the door in his face and looked at Margo. We both laughed.

"I really hope they consider it," Margo said as she picked up her yoga mat, rolled it and put it against one of the walls. "It's such an amazing experience."

I checked my phone. There were still a few minutes before our two roommates were due to arrive.

"Well, I'd love to hear the story."

She sat down at her make-up mirror and began twirling her hair into pin curls.

"I had a hysterectomy in my twenties because of uterine fibroids, but I knew I wanted children so I harvested my eggs. Having a surrogate meant Andy and I could have a baby who was biologically ours even if I couldn't get pregnant. We worked with an agency and found the loveliest woman. She really wanted us to be an active part of the pregnancy. We were there for all the appointments—the agency had a whole medical clinic right on site—and Andy was always trying to anticipate what her next craving might be. The poor thing probably still has cupboards filled with pickles and chocolate-covered gummy bears."

"It must have been so exciting to see Nora being born."

"Well, I actually didn't get to. We got the call that Lily was in labour, but by the time we got there, she'd already given birth."

"Couldn't wait to meet you, I guess."

"That's what Lily said."

Margo prattled on until the other actresses arrived and started getting ready. I quietly excused myself and slipped into the corridor. I really didn't see how surrogacy would figure into the case, but it was an avenue Jeffers and I hadn't explored and I wondered if it might be worth considering.

I found Adam in the green room waiting for the kettle to boil.

"Hey, did Margo tell you the name of the surrogacy agency she used?"

Adam looked at me, eyes wide, mouth open ready to squeal.

"Not for me," I said, cutting off any jubilation he was ready to let loose.

"Oh," he said, downcast.

I fumbled through an explanation. "A friend and … his wife have been trying and … maybe this might be … um, something … they might find interesting."

"But, just to be clear, this 'friend' is not Paul and 'his wife' is not you?"

"That's right."

"Is it your hot cop friend?"

"Jeffers? Jeffers isn't hot. He's…"

"Hot."

"Oh my god."

"He's totally got a Ryan Phillippe/Jude Law kind of vibe. You know with the—"

"I don't know and I don't need to and no, he doesn't," I said, wanting to bring an end to the conversation as quickly as possible. "So, the agency?"

"Yeah, she gave me a brochure," he said, pulling a pamphlet out of the pile he had amassed in my dressing room and handing it to me. "She gave me a few. You can keep it."

"Thank you," I said.

The cover had a picture of a baby nestled in the protective bowl of a white lotus flower while the words SEEDLINGS ADOPTION and SURROGACY SERVICES and NATAL CLINIC swirled around the image.

"You know, come to think of it, there might even be a smidge of Ryan Seacrest in there," Adam said.

"What are you looking at?" Jeffers asked the following day as we headed out of Niagara-on-the-Lake toward Niagara Falls and Molly's Garden.

"Nothing," I said.

"You keep staring at me."

Adam had insisted on scrolling through numerous photos trying to convince me of Jeffers' celebrity likeness. In the end I had conceded that Jeffers' bone structure shared some similarities with the Ryans and Mr. Law but I had refused to comment on whether those features earned Jeffers the official distinction of being deemed "hot."

Now, face to face with the man in question, I was trying to come to a more informed conclusion.

"Do I have mustard on my face again?"

"Why would you be eating mustard this early in the morning?"

"Aden likes it with his bacon."

"Ew."

"Right? I don't know where he picked that up. We're hoping he grows out of it. Unfortunately, this morning he wanted to be the airplane and feed Daddy, but he kept missing the runway, as it were. Anyway, I thought I got most of it off."

Jeffers started wiping madly at his face, stealing a glance at himself in the rear-view mirror.

"You're fine. Never mind. Listen, what about surrogacy?"

"What about it? Isn't that what we've been investigating?"

"Well, yeah. I mean, we think the missing women are being used as surrogates, but I'm wondering if the baby ring is operating under the cover of a surrogacy agency?"

I quickly filled Jeffers in on Margo Livingston's experience.

"I know there's nothing in her story that's at all suspicious, but her surrogate's name was Lily, which is similar to Milla, and my mind just went … I don't know."

We drove in silence for several minutes.

"It would be hard to profit from surrogacy," Jeffers said. "Surrogate mothers are only allowed to receive compensation for directly related expenses and consultants or agencies can't be paid to match surrogates with parents or manage the pregnancy. The laws are very strict."

"That may be, but we've already determined the people we're looking for are not operating within the confines of the law. So, given that, couldn't an agency offer an all-inclusive service to parents? Facilitate the match, arrange medical visits, basically oversee the whole process from beginning to end and maybe inflate the costs along the way just a bit?"

"Ye-es," Jeffers said, hesitantly. "But there are lawyers involved as well to—"

"Oh, like there's never been a lawyer on the take."

"Bella, I really ... okay, yes. It's possible. I guess," Jeffers said finally. "But the bond that develops between a surrogate and the parents is a part of the process that is so important to all the people involved. Your friend even said how rewarding that was. So, if a girl or woman is being held against her will, it would be risky to have her form close relationships with prospective parents."

"Unless all meetings with the parents are supervised."

Jeffers nodded as he considered this.

"Or they aren't being held against their will."

"I can't believe that," Jeffers said.

"Think about it. Milla ran away. She was living on the street and trying to hide from Kieran. If someone approached her and offered her a place to live, meals, safety and all she'd have to do in return was have a few babies...?"

"Okay. I'll give you Milla. But what about Angela? Keesha? Bernadelle? That profile doesn't fit them."

"I know," I said. "I just got this feeling when Margo was talking yesterday and … but, you're right. It's too far-fetched."

"There are a lot, and I mean a lot, of checks in place when it comes to surrogacy. I just don't see how the ring could manage it."

"How do you know so much about surrogacy anyway?"

"Aria's brother and his wife used one. Had a fantastic experience."

"Yeah, same with Margo and Andy," I said, conceding the point and slouching in my seat. "Unfortunately, there's nothing fantastic about what happened to Milla and the others."

Chapter 19

Our timing was terrible. Again. Just as we had descended upon Zees in the middle of their dinner rush, we arrived at Molly's Garden as they were serving breakfast. A volunteer directed us to Sister Ruth, who had far less patience and far fewer manners than Ross but who, nonetheless, provided the information we needed.

"Kelly's Refrigerated Delivery," Jeffers said, reading the business card the sister had given us before hustling us out of the building.

A quick Google search gave us an address, and twenty minutes later we pulled up in front of a long, industrial building that housed several small businesses. Kelly's was on the end and obvious because two company trucks were parked out front.

"Yes? What can I do you for?" asked a heavily moustached, senior gentleman sitting behind a desk in the small office. His welcome was warm and his voice jolly.

Jeffers showed his badge. "We have a few questions about an ongoing investigation. We're hoping you can help us."

"Don't imagine I can but I'm happy to try. Leroy Kelly," the man said with an emphasis on the second syllable of his first name. He extended his hand and shook mine and Jeffers' in turn. "Why don't I get us some tea and you can tell me what this is all about."

He crossed to a small counter on the other side of the room where a kettle, a microwave and bar fridge made up a very basic kitchenette.

I had never met either of my grandfathers, but my father's mother, Terri-Mae, had often talked about her husband, Campbell—after whom I was named—as a big teddy bear of a man, kind to everyone he met, and ready to move heaven and earth if it would help you. Leroy's eyes, smile, and voice all exuded kindness and I guessed he was similar.

"Tell me about your operation," Jeffers said.

"Kelly's has been in business over a hundred years."

"A hundred years?" I asked.

"My old man was an iceman like his old man and his grandfather before him. He made the move to refrigeration along with everyone else. Me and my brother came on board as soon as we were old enough to work. We only had one truck then but plenty of work to keep us busy. When Daddy died, we added a second truck, and when my brother died, I added a third. Two for his boys and one for my sister's son."

"So, it's still a real family business," I said.

"Yes, ma'am. Now," he said, returning to the desk with cups of tea, "why don't you tell me what brings you folks here today." He pulled an open package of Peek Freans out of a desk drawer and shook a selection onto a plate.

"You transport food that needs to be kept cold or frozen, is that correct?"

"Yes. But we also move pharmaceuticals, tobacco, cosmetics, chemicals, even artwork. Anything that needs to be in a temperature-controlled environment to prevent spoiling."

"I … I had no idea," Jeffers said, genuinely surprised.

"Now you do," Leroy said, smiling.

He offered the plate of cookies. Jeffers and I both refused but he helped himself to one.

"Well, we're interested in a delivery you did for Molly's Garden."

"The soup kitchen in Niagara Falls?"

"That's the one."

"We do a lot of soup kitchens," Leroy said, sipping his tea. "Was there a complaint? They haven't mentioned anything to us. We have a good relationship. If there's ever anything—"

"It's nothing like that," Jeffers said. "And actually, we're looking at a delivery that would have taken place about a year ago."

"Gosh. Well, the memory isn't as good as it used to be but she's still okay. What do you want to know?"

"Basically, we'd just like to speak to whoever picked up the Molly's Garden food donation from Zees restaurant. A woman who worked there went missing shortly thereafter and we think one of your guys might have been one of the last people to have seen her."

Leroy's brow furrowed and he leaned back in his chair, crossing his arms.

He had mentioned his employees were his nephews, and he looked alarmed that we were suggesting one of these boys might be responsible for a woman's disappearance.

"We're wondering whether she might have said something about where she was headed next," I said, hoping to alleviate his fears. "We're just trying to piece together a timeline."

Leroy's shoulders visibly relaxed and his brow smoothed.

"She's been missing a year, you said?"

"A little over," Jeffers answered.

"Awful thing."

"Yes."

"It was probably Cam. He does most of the local deliveries. You got a date?"

Jeffers gave Leroy the particulars, and the older man tapped them into the old desktop computer that sat on the corner of his desk.

"Yeah, as I thought," Leroy said, turning the screen so Jeffers and I could see.

"Cameron Monroe?"

"My sister's boy. Good kid. Actually, not much of a kid anymore. Getting married soon. Can hardly believe it. He's a great worker."

"We'd love to have a quick word with him," Jeffers said. "Is he around? Or will he be back soon?"

"He's off today. But if you give me your number, I'll see he gets in touch."

"Thank you," Jeffers said, retrieving a card from his wallet and placing it on the desk. He stood to go.

"Mr. Kelly," I said, maintaining my seat, "you mentioned you serve a number of soup kitchens?"

"That's right."

I looked to Jeffers, who smiled and gave me a nod. "How far back do your records go? And may we have copies?"

With Jeffers' help, Leroy had managed to email the records to Steven. While they were currently being checked for deliveries to the Salvation Army food bank where Bernadelle Klassen had volunteered and the soup kitchen from which Angela Hansen had gone missing, Jeffers and I took the scenic route to Vineland and Kieran Martin's mysterious property.

Kieran hadn't been kidding when he said the house wasn't ready for visitors. From where Jeffers and I stood in the driveway, we could see spots where the shingles on the roof were loose or missing, the covered porch was in need of levelling, and the most recent paint job was peeling considerably, revealing that the house had once been blue.

We could also see what had likely drawn Kieran to the property. The house was large enough to easily accommodate a home practice, it was situated on plenty of land, and despite being in need of repair, it had a traditional, country charm. Decorative mouldings and trim, large, shuttered windows, and enormous chimney running up one side.

"This would be perfect to use for a movie," I said.

"Hopefully not a horror film," Jeffers said.

His phone rang before we could get out of the car.

"Jeffers."

There was moment of silence on the line followed by a hesitant voice, "Uh, yeah, is this Detective Sergeant Andre Jeffers?"

"It is," Jeffers said.

"This is Cameron Monroe. My uncle said you needed to speak with me?"

Cameron's voice was deep and smooth. Soothing. My initial thought was that it was wasted in his current job; his true calling was something like a therapist. Or a hypnotist.

"Thanks for calling back so quickly, Cameron."

"My uncle said it might be important."

"Yes. And just to let you know, I have you on speaker phone. My partner is here as well."

"That's fine."

"Cameron, do you remember a pick-up you did about a year ago from Zees restaurant in Niagara-on-the-Lake? It was a food donation for Molly's Garden."

"I guess. I've been doing that run once a week for a couple of years now," Cameron said.

"So, you would remember Keesha Rodrigues? She was a manager at the restaurant."

Cameron was silent.

"She's the one who went missing," he said, after a moment.

"That's right," Jeffers said.

We waited for Cameron to respond. When he didn't, Jeffers continued.

"We think you might have been one of the last people to see her before she disappeared and we're wondering if she said anything that would give us an idea of where she might have gone after she left the restaurant."

We could hear Cameron breathing on the line but, otherwise, he remained silent.

"If you can remember anything at all," I said. "Even if it seems insignificant to you."

"I'm trying," Cameron said.

"I'm sorry," I said. "I didn't mean to rush you."

"I wish I could remember something helpful. But we didn't really talk about … anything, you know. Just about the order. We used to talk more, but then she was gone for a bit and when she came back, she was … quieter. She was still nice and everything, but she wasn't chatty like she had been. I liked her. I was shocked when I heard what happened."

"How did she seem the last time you saw her?" Jeffers asked.

"I dunno. Kinda sad, I guess."

"But she didn't say why?"

A pause. "No."

"Okay. Thank you, Cameron. If you do remember anything, you have my number."

"Sure," he said, before hanging up.

"Well, so much for that," Jeffers said, exiting the car.

I followed and together we climbed the steps that led to the main entrance.

The front door was open behind a wooden screen door. Together we peered through the dusty mesh into the house's interior.

"Looks like the inside needs as much work as the outside," I said.

"According to the paperwork I saw, he got a great deal on this place. I can see why."

Jeffers knocked and simultaneously called out a hello. I walked the length of the porch and peeked around one side the house. There were large, roped off areas where the soil had already been turned over. In each of these areas a complex grid had been carefully mapped out and plotted.

Jeffers knocked again.

"There's no one around the side," I said, rejoining Jeffers at the door.

He opened the screen door and stepped inside. "Hello?"

The old character of the place took my breath away. The few existing walls rose to meet high ceilings and boasted wide baseboards and crown moulding that managed to be both elegant and distinguished. The wood floors bore evidence of years of traffic. A few new walls had been framed and roughed in and I hoped the renovation would honour the splendour that had once, obviously, existed throughout.

"I'm going this way," Jeffers said and pointed down a hallway.

"Okay. I'll check out the kitchen."

Neither of us had taken more than a couple of steps when a thump overhead caught our attention.

Jeffers brought a finger to his lips.

There was a second thump. Then a third.

Jeffers and I moved slowly to the base of the stairs and began a silent ascent.

The second floor of the house looked much like the first, although it was slightly further along in its restoration.

The thumping continued.

We followed the sound to a room at the end of the corridor and stopped just outside the open door.

"Mr. Martin?" Jeffers called. "It's Detective Sergeant Andre Jeffers. I'm sorry to barge in. I did knock."

There was silence followed by a short, whispered conversation I was unable to make out.

"Mr. Martin?"

"Um … he's not here," a hesitant voice said.

A moment later, a bearded man in jeans and a sweat-stained T-shirt stepped into the hall.

"Is there something I can help you with?"

"And you are?"

"Ken Hernder. I'm doing the work here."

"Nice to meet you," Jeffers said. "Looks like you have your work cut out for you. Do you mind if we take a look?"

Ken moved out of the way to let us pass.

We entered what I guessed would become one of the bedrooms. There were buckets of drywall compound in one corner and sheets of drywall leaning against one of the walls. A large window was open, and a man as bearded and as sweaty as Ken was standing on some kind of platform on the exterior side. I managed to catch of glimpse of his phone being tucked into his back pocket.

"We bring things for the upper level in through here," Ken said, indicating the window. "It's easier than lugging them up all those stairs."

"You got a winch?" Jeffers asked.

Ken stifled a snicker. "It's … uh … a hydraulic scaffold."

"Fancy."

"Yeah."

Ken stood nervously in the middle of the room looking at the floor. His colleague sat on the windowsill picking dirt out of his fingernails. Jeffers did a turn of the space, inspecting its contents. And I leaned up against the door frame not knowing what to do with my hands.

"I told Kieran we might be stopping by," Jeffers said eventually, breaking the awkward silence. "Just want to take a look around."

"O-kay," said Ken. "He never mentioned it. He usually doesn't want—"

"You guys carry on," Jeffers said with a smile. "Don't let us stop you. We'll just give ourselves the tour. We promise not to disturb anything."

"Um…"

Jeffers looked at Ken calmly, still smiling, eyebrows raised, waiting for a reply.

Ken had the good sense not to challenge him.

We had no legal grounds for being there, but it was clear neither Ken nor his buddy knew that.

"Very good," Jeffers said and indicated, with an outstretched arm directed at me, that we should go on our way.

We stepped into the hallway but managed to hear Ken's associate whisper, "Oh man. K's gonna kill you," and Ken's "Shut up. What was I supposed to do?" before we were out of earshot.

"I imagine we only have about ten minutes or so before Kieran shows up," Jeffers said quietly. "I'm pretty sure the scaffold man texted him."

"You saw that, too?" I said. Jeffers nodded. "So, where do we start?"

"You check the rest of the rooms up here. See if there's attic access in any of them and, if there is, go up. But be careful. In old homes like this, the floor isn't always reinforced. I'll check the ground floor and the basement. If he's hiding something, or … god forbid, someone, they're going to be tucked away somewhere."

I nodded.

"And be quick," he said. "If we see something worth investigating, I'll get a team out here. We only have time for a hasty once-over."

Five minutes later we met in the kitchen and compared notes.

"The attic is accessible through the ceiling in one of the closets in the master bedroom. It's pretty big, but I didn't see anything but lot of insulation," I reported.

"Nothing down here either. Dammit. I was so sure he was hiding something. I mean, the way he reacted when I ment—"

Jeffers stopped speaking mid-thought as he gazed out a window at the acreage beyond.

"What is it?"

"Do you see that?" he asked, pointing his finger.

I followed the path his finger made to a door in the ground several feet away.

"Is that a storm cellar?"

Chapter 20

"Detective Jeffers!" Kieran's voice rang out across the yard.

Jeffers was bent over the storm door, gripping the handle. He cursed under his breath, released his grasp, and straightened up just as Kieran finished his run toward us.

"Mr. Martin, quite a place you've got here. Your crew was good enough to let us take a little tour. I was just about to show my partner here your storm cellar. She's a city girl. Only ever seen one of these in the movies."

"I really just use it for storage," Kieran said, out of breath. "There's not much to see down there, I'm afraid."

"Well, then, we won't be disturbing anything," Jeffers said. "Lead the way."

Kieran took a few cautious steps toward the door then planted himself firmly on top, completely blocking our access. I could see his knees shaking through his pants and wondered if holding his ground like this was the bravest thing he had ever done.

"Mr. Martin, let me explain this clearly. If you do not let us down there, I will call for a warrant, and if you think that will buy you some time to move whatever it is you're hiding, you're mistaken. My partner and I will stand on these very spots until the warrant is delivered. At which time this will become an official investigation and anything we find goes on record. Now, if you were to voluntarily show us around, I could choose to turn a blind eye to whatever I might see, just like I have so far with the permits that are missing for the work being done on the house."

Kieran lowered his eyes. "I … I'll … they're…"

"Kieran."

"I can explain."

"Why don't you show us instead?"

Kieran's eyes met Jeffers. Met mine. They were imploring us to let this go. His mouth moved in a wordless plea. Whatever he had in the cellar was either incredibly valuable to him or something that could get him into a lot of trouble. Maybe both.

Jeffers pulled out his phone.

"Okay!" Kieran said. "But you have to know, I don't want to hurt anyone. That's not why I have them."

"Kieran, the door," Jeffers said, urgency colouring his words.

He nodded and lifted the hatch. After descending a couple of steps, he stopped and turned to us. "Please don't touch anything. Please."

I followed Jeffers down the wooden steps and I saw him unclip the holster of his gun. The cellar was deeper than I had imagined and the steps were steep. Kieran waited for us in a small hallway with two metal doors on either side.

"Unlock the doors," Jeffers ordered. "Then stand back against the wall with your hands where I can see them."

The sound of his voice was all but swallowed by the depth.

A small whimper escaped from Kieran but he did as he was told.

The room on the left was brightly lit by racks of hanging lamps simulating sunlight. I could also hear a fan somewhere in the room. Growing out of large planters on the ground were two-foot-high stalks—some with flowers on the ends and some in their pre-bloom state with gray-green buds at their tips. The flowers were mostly red, but some were so deep in colour they looked almost purple.

The second room was darker. It smelled earthy. There were tables set up with trays of mushrooms in various stages of growth.

"What is all this?" Jeffers asked.

"Poppies," Kieran said, quietly.

"Poppies?"

"And mushrooms."

"I can see that," Jeffers said. "Why were you so afraid to show us a few flowers and some mushrooms?"

Kieran opened his mouth but made no sound.

"Jeffers, I think they might be magic mushrooms," I said.

Jeffers looked to Kieran, who nodded.

"And the poppies?" Jeffers asked.

"Opi … opium poppies."

"I'm sorry," Jeffers said, "did you say 'opium'?"

Kieran nodded again.

"You're growing plants for narcotics?"

"No!" Kieran said.

"Well, that's what it looks like to me," Jeffers said as his phone made another appearance.

"Don't! Please, let me explain."

Jeffers looked to me.

"Go ahead, Kieran," I said.

"The poppies are used—"

"To make heroin," Jeffers interrupted.

"Yes. That's true. But they're used for other things as well."

"Oh yeah?"

"They're used as pain killers and to induce sleep. It can dramatically increase the comfort of people who suffer from chronic pain and cancer... The mushrooms—there have been a lot of clinical studies that show how they can be used to treat depression and anxiety. They're only bad if abused. If they're used properly, both of these plants have the power to drastically improve quality of life.

"It's like how LSD was used in the sixties. It had been proven to be an effective treatment for schizophrenia and alcoholism, but all that was overshadowed by its recreational use. Eventually, all the research and ... advancements stopped."

Kieran had grown more emotional the more he talked. And the more he talked, the depth of his passion for his vocation became clearer.

"I know they're narcotics, Detective. And I know it's illegal to grow them. But I'm not selling them for any kind of leisure use. They are very powerful medicines, and there are people who need them. People in extreme circumstances who find little relief elsewhere. People who are just trying to live as normal a life as possible. I can give them that. And I don't think that's such a bad thing."

I looked at Jeffers. His face betrayed nothing of what he was thinking. The complete opposite of Kieran.

"Milla called you from Keesha Rodrigues' phone," Jeffers said after a painfully long silence. "How did Keesha have your number?"

Kieran stammered. It was obviously not what he was expecting Jeffers to say.

"Do you know Keesha Rodrigues?"

"No," Kieran said when he managed to get his mouth back in working order. "I have no idea how she had my number. Maybe—she—maybe she came into the clinic?"

"But she wasn't a regular client?"

"No."

"Do you keep records of all your transactions?"

"We do. And … and I will check as soon as I get back to the office."

Jeffers nodded. He fixed his stare on Kieran and the young herbalist inhaled and held his breath.

"We spoke with Milla's sister," Jeffers said. "Evidently Milla did go by the house four years ago like she told you she was going to."

Kieran's eyes widened and he hung on Jeffers' every word.

"Milla said some guy was harassing her. That she was scared of him and needed her sister's help to get rid of him."

"What? Why wouldn't she have told me? I would have…" Kieran's voice trailed off as the realization hit him. "Me?"

"Sarah just said it was someone with the initial 'K.'"

Kieran slid down the wall and came to rest on the rough ground. "She's lying. We loved each other. We…"

A tear fell down his cheek. Kieran removed his glasses and wiped his eyes with his sleeve.

"She also said Milla was stoned."

"What? No. No, no, no, no. Milla was clean. She hadn't touched that stuff in ages. She's lying. Milla wouldn't. She's lying."

"You're the one who spoke with Sarah. What do you think?" Jeffers asked when we were back in the car.

We'd left an upset Kieran with a warning to get his building permits. There had been no mention of his illegal plants.

"I think she was telling the truth. I also think Kieran's telling the truth."

"They both can't be."

"Why not? What if Milla ran into an old friend? Someone she knew from the street. Or her old dealer. Maybe she thought a little hit of something wouldn't hurt. Might boost her courage before the job interview. Before seeing her family."

"But why make up all the stuff about Kieran hassling her?"

"She probably knew she couldn't go home to him in the state she was in. Maybe she was ashamed. Or maybe she knew how hard it would be to get clean again, and rather than let Kieran see her like that, she figured she'd break it off."

"By making up a story to get her sister to do it for her. Hmmm, I don't know. That's a lot of maybes."

Jeffers phone rang. It was Steven. He hit the Bluetooth button and answered.

"What have you got?" Jeffers asked.

"Okay, there was a delivery to the soup kitchen here in town on the day Angela Hansen went missing. There are also regular deliveries to the Sally Ann in Fort Erie where the Klassen woman volunteered."

"That was fast. There were years of records."

"Just got to punch the right information into the computer and then let it do the work. There's something else. Lindsey's been working the food bank angle and, sure enough, we can connect four other missing women to such establishments."

"And are they served by Kelly's?"

"They sure are. The dates of their disappearances match delivery dates and times."

"And how far back do these dates go?" Jeffers asked.

"About ten years. It seems as if Bernadelle Klassen might have been the first."

Jeffers inhaled deeply and closed his eyes. "Okay," he said. "Same delivery guy?"

"Yessir. A Mr. Cameron Monroe."

Jeffers exhaled loudly and pursed his lips. "This is good work, Steven. Thank you."

"You want me to run a check on him?"

"Yes. And on Kelly's Refrigerated Delivery."

"You got it."

A chime from Jeffers' phone indicated Steven had hung up. We sat in the silence that followed.

Jeffers started the car and I checked the clock on the dashboard. Moustache would be getting antsy for a snack.

"Kelly's is really the only game in town for that kind of service. Might just be a coincidence," I said into the quiet of the car.

Jeffers nodded.

"Might not."

Jeffers nodded again.

"What are you thinking?"

"I'm thinking I'd like to get to know Mr. Monroe a little better."

"You going to call him in?"

"I need to talk to Lindsey and Crayne." He blew out an exasperated breath. "Where are we at with Arnold Reymer?"

"We're seeing him today after Paul's finished at the clinic. I called him right before you picked me up. Just as you predicted, he was anxious to get us in as soon as possible. He offered to see us first thing this morning. I think he's actually staying late tonight to accommodate us."

"Excellent. Hopefully tonight's meeting will clarify a few things."

Chapter 21

Arnold Reymer ushered us into his office with a pomp and circumstance that would have embarrassed the Queen then sat behind his desk, his back rod straight and eyes expectant.

"We're sorry for keeping you here so late," I said. "Thank you so much for making the time for us."

"I don't mind at all," Arnold said. "It gave me a chance to get caught up on some paperwork. I gather you've made a decision?"

"We have."

"Excellent." He opened a file on his desk and lifted his pen.

"I'm afraid," Paul said, "that while your offer is tempting, we're going to have to decline."

Arnold stiffened and his smile faltered ever so slightly. "I'm sorry?"

"We've given it a lot of thought," I said. "And it's not about the money or even the risk. There simply isn't a guarantee at the end of the day."

I watched Arnold fight to keep his composure as the meeting ventured further and further away from what he had been expecting.

"There's still a chance we won't be matched. And there's still a chance that, if we are matched, the mother will change her mind."

"And then there's the timing," Paul said, continuing our rehearsed response. "You mentioned how long the adoption process can take. Even without a record. And we simply don't want to wait."

Arnold nodded and relaxed the hold on his pen.

"We want to explore other options that might not have as much of a time factor," I said.

"And what options are those?" he asked.

"Well, we're not entirely sure, offhand. It's something we need to research."

"I see."

I inhaled and squeezed Paul's hand, never taking my eyes off Arnold's face. This would be the moment when he'd decide whether to present his less profitable option.

"I … understand," he said, closing the file on his desk. His posture eased into the smug stuffiness that had been evident at our first meeting.

We waited for him to continue.

He didn't.

"Well, thank you," I said, rising. "We're sorry to have wasted your time. I suppose we could have told you our decision over the phone."

"Mmmm, yes," he said.

His eyes moved back and forth from me to Paul as if in careful consideration.

I smiled, hoping to cover the disappointment that was, surely, seeping through my pores. Either Arnold Reymer wasn't part of the baby ring in any way, or he hadn't deemed us worthy enough to invite us into the fold. I guessed it was the latter and kicked myself internally for getting so close but not delivering what Morris had put me on the case to achieve.

Paul stood to join me and extended his hand to Arnold.

"Have you thought about surrogacy?" Arnold asked.

Paul and I looked at each other and resumed our seats and Arnold slid a brochure with a picture of a baby nestled in a white lotus flower across his desk.

"It's the same service my friend used," I told Jeffers over the phone when we'd returned to the car. "It's called Seedlings. They handle adoptions and also provide all of the health care for surrogates up to and including the birth."

"Well, as I said, the surrogacy process is hard to corrupt. But if Arnold is getting paid for referrals, something is definitely off. Do you think your friend—"

"No," I said. "I don't think Margo would have been so forthcoming about the experience if she'd been involved in anything illegal. Besides her daughter looks just like her and her husband. There's no way she … bought her."

"Okay, we've got to get in there if we're going to learn anything for certain."

"We have an appointment tomorrow. First thing in the morning."

"Wow."

"Arnold made a call and set it up," I said.

"And probably just earned himself a cool twenty-five thousand. Okay, I'm going to bring this to Lindsey. This place, Seedlings, hasn't been on our radar whatsoever, so we need to do some digging and come up with a plan. In the meantime, treat tomorrow as an information-gathering session. Get as many details as you can and act very interested in all of them. Even though you're not going to make any commitment tomorrow, I want them to know you're serious. I want them to believe they can hook you into whatever their game is."

Paul nodded.

"All right," I said, answering for both of us. "Anything on Cameron Monroe or Kelly's?"

"Both clean. That doesn't mean there's no connection. It just means we haven't found it."

"Yet," I said.

"I like your optimism. Oh, and get this. Kieran called earlier. Said there was no record of Keesha Rodrigues ever visiting the clinic. Still claimed not to have any idea how she would have gotten his number."

"Given what we know about what he's growing, it would be pretty stupid of him to lie to us," I said.

Jeffers nodded. "Two for two, Samuel. First the Kelly records and now this assessment. I'd almost think you were a real detective."

Out of the corner of my eye, I saw Paul's shoulders stiffen.

"What's going to happen to Arnold?" I asked.

"That's up to Lindsey," Jeffers said. "And, for the next hour, I'm not going to think about him or this case or anything. I'm going to put Aden to bed and have a quick dinner with my wife before I head back to the station."

"Lucky you. What did she make tonight?"

"You really want to know?"

"Please," Paul said from the driver's seat. "Let us live vicariously through you. Our big plan is to ask Moustache to share some of his supper."

I laughed. "Yeah, like that would ever happen."

"Eating dog food?" Jeffers asked.

"Moustache sharing."

"Please, what magical dish did Aria create out of thin air?" Paul asked.

"Grilled salmon with a chorizo-olive sauce, roasted fingerling potatoes, and grilled garlic parmesan asparagus."

Paul and I shared an envious look.

"Well, according to the can, there's salmon in Moustache's food too," I said.

"Salmon, venison, and halibut," Paul added.

"Sounds like we're all in for a bit of a feast tonight," Jeffers said. "Listen, you guys did great today. Let me know how it goes tomorrow. Keep your eyes open. Don't let anything go unnoticed."

Chapter 22

The picture caught my eye immediately.

I nodded at what seemed like a never-ending barrage of information, all the while waiting to ask, "Is that your son?"

Valerie Kinsey looked at the picture to which I had referred. "Yes," she said, proudly. "And before you ask, he was not born via surrogate," she added with a laugh.

Paul and I had been at Seedlings for about half an hour, having been treated to cappuccino and fresh scones in one of the three family rooms where prospective parents and the pregnant women would meet, followed by a tour of the facility.

There were two fully outfitted exam rooms and one delivery room as well as a comfortable ward with two beds for families and expectant women to wait out the labour.

"Every moment, from conception to delivery, happens right here," Valerie had told us. "We have an excellent obstetrics team."

There was even a small, industrial kitchen complete with a chef so that surrogates and families could enjoy a visit over a gourmet lunch.

We were now sitting in Valerie's office where she was outlining the details of the surrogacy process.

I excused myself to go to the washroom leaving Paul, with a puzzled look on his face, to continue the mission.

"Jeffers," I whispered into my phone when I was certain I was alone.

"What's going on? I thought you were at Seedlings?"

"We are and—"

"Why are you whispering? Is everything okay?"

"No," I said. "The owner's son is Sarah's fiancé."

Jeffers was silent.

"Milla's sister, Sarah, is engaged to the owner's son," I repeated.

"Are you sure?"

"I'm positive. I recognized him right away. It took me a minute to remember where I knew him from, but then it came to me. The press conference. He was standing with Sarah when you made the announcement about Milla's death."

I heard Jeffers start typing.

"The owner's name is Valerie Kinsey," I said.

"Yes, I know. I have it in front of me. Give me a second."

"Jeffers, I have to get back in there."

"Yeah, you do. And after what I'm about to tell you, you're going to need to put your acting skills into high gear. Do you think you can do that?"

"Just tell me."

"Valerie Kinsey's maiden name is Kelly."

"And?"

"As in Leroy Kelly."

I gasped. "Leroy's sister?"

"Yup. And about thirty years ago, she was married briefly to a man named David Monroe."

"Oh my god," I said.

"Making her son—"

"Cameron," we said together.

"I never got his name at the press conference," Jeffers said. "He was introduced as Sarah's boyfriend. And the only contact I've had with him since has been on the phone. I had no reason to suspect the two men were one and the same. Dammit."

"We have to tell Sarah. And the Koeppers," I said.

"Tell them what?" Jeffers asked. "We don't know anything definitive. But we definitely have enough to call him in. And his ties to the natal clinic certainly don't look good. Once we have a chance to question him—"

"It might be too late," I finished. "When he realizes we're on to him, and if he did have something to do with Milla's death, Sarah could be in danger."

Jeffers sighed.

"Sarah told me she brought Milla to her boyfriend's place after she showed up at the house. She said Milla took off a few days later. But what if she didn't? What if Cameron took her somewhere? The same place he took Angela and Bernadelle. The same place Keesha's been for over a year. Sarah connects Cameron to Milla. He'd try to get her out of the way."

"Bella, there's still so much we don't know—it's possible Cameron isn't involved at all."

"Do you really believe that?"

"It doesn't matter what I believe. What matters is that protocols need to be followed in cases like this, and if they're not followed correctly, that could be what decides whether a person is put away and punished or whether the whole thing is thrown out on a technicality."

It was my turn to sigh. Jeffers was right.

"Besides," Jeffers continued, "Cameron is, essentially, part of Sarah's family. Best not to cast doubt until we're sure. It could do a lot of damage."

"So, what do we do?"

"You are going to go back into your meeting, and I am going to track down Mr. Monroe. With any luck, one of us will learn something helpful."

"Anything I can do?" Jarod Riley asked from the doorway of my dressing room.

I had a generous chunk of time where I didn't appear on stage during *Arms and the Man*. Jarod played Nicola, the head servant of the household and fiancé to my Louka, and as most of our scenes were together, it unfortunately meant he did too.

"Hmmm?" I said, looking up from resting my head in my hands.

"Everything okay?"

"Yeah, I just had a really busy morning and I've got some things to go over," I said.

"The script for the director's project? It's good, isn't it? I was disappointed Matt wasn't able to use me in the end, but I think Ginny's play is better. I'm glad she asked me. We've got a couple of steamy scenes."

The casting had been announced the day before, and I'd been surprised to discover Jarod and I had been cast as lovers. I don't know what he did to get out of his arrangement with Matt and into one with Ginny, but I was certain he'd had a hand in how things ended up.

"I haven't had a chance to read it yet, actually. I've got a few other things that need my attention," I said, indicating the goody bag of literature we had taken away from our meeting at Seedlings, which sat on my lap.

As I shifted in my seat, one of the pamphlets fell to the floor. Jarod rushed to pick it up as I bent over to retrieve it, and we narrowly avoided a collision.

"Goodness," he said, as he saw the pamphlet's cover.

"It's not what you think," I said. He raised his eyebrows. "I'm just doing a bit of research for … a … film that I've been…"

"Ah, gotcha," he said with a knowing wink. "I know. Film people can be so secretive about their upcoming projects."

"Yeah," I said, shrugging apologetically about not being able to be more forthcoming.

"Well, I'll leave you to it. Very exciting. Perhaps, when you're allowed to talk about it, you can give me all the juicy details over drinks," he said, handing the pamphlet back to me.

One of the photos on the back caught my eye and, in my shock, I inadvertently agreed to Jarod's proposal.

I barely noticed him leave. My world view shrank until all I could see was the photo and the words beneath it. It was a testimonial from one of Valerie's surrogates, gushing about her experience with Seedlings. According to the pamphlet, the woman's name was Shona Murphy but her face was unmistakably Sarah Ward's.

Chapter 23

"I don't understand," Sarah said, looking at the photograph and shaking her head.

I had called Jeffers during the intermission, and he was waiting by the stage door when the show ended. We arrived at the Koeppers' house twenty-five minutes later.

"So, you've never worked as a surrogate for Ms. Kinsey?" Jeffers asked.

"Of course not!"

Sarah looked to her aunt, who was seated next to her on the sofa in their living room. Ellen patted her knee and squeezed her hand. Rodney stood by the fireplace a few feet away with his arms crossed.

"Cameron took this picture right after we got engaged. I couldn't stop smiling and he wanted to capture that. He has it in a frame in his room. I can't believe Valerie would do something like this."

"There has to be some explanation," Ellen said. "I mean, it's obviously a mistake. Someone printed the wrong photo.

I bet Valerie didn't even notice. She would have said something to Sarah, I'm sure of it."

"Sweetie, why don't you call her and straighten this out?" Rodney said.

"Mr. Koepper," Jeffers said, "would you mind taking a seat?"

"I don't like the sound of this," Rodney said, moving to sit next to his wife.

"We have some new information," Jeffers said.

"About Milla? You've found who—"

"Not yet, I'm afraid. And, I'm sorry, but I can't really give you too many details about the lead we're following."

"But you have a lead?" Sarah asked.

"We do."

"Okay. Good," Rodney said, putting his arm around Ellen. "Well, that's something. That's closer than you've been."

"Yes," Jeffers agreed.

"So, what is it? The lead?"

"I want you to understand that it is very early yet. *Very* early. We don't have a lot of information, and the little we do have might not take us anywhere."

"Okay," Sarah said, "but—" She was cut off by the buzzing of her phone. "It's Cameron," she said, looking at the screen.

I looked at Jeffers. He had called Cameron into the station while I'd been doing my matinee. Apparently, the young man had been cooperative but not a great source of information. According to Jeffers, Cameron hadn't disputed the delivery records we'd taken from Kelly's, but, except for Keesha Rodrigues, he hadn't copped to knowing any of the other women. It was what Jeffers had expected him to say, of course, and he had no choice but to let Cameron go.

"There's more he's not telling us. I'm sure of it," Jeffers had said to me in the car on the way to the Koeppers.

I figured it was only a matter of time before Cameron called Sarah to tell her about what happened. I was surprised it had taken this long.

Sarah's phone buzzed again.

"Not now, Sarah. You can call him back," Rodney said.

"Sarah, how long have you known Cameron Monroe?" Jeffers asked.

"What? Why?"

"Please just answer the question."

Sarah looked to her aunt and uncle before answering. "Almost five years."

"And how well do you know his mother, Valerie?"

"Why are you asking me these things?"

I could see she was starting to get upset.

"Sarah," I said, "the new information we have directly relates to Valerie's business, Seedlings."

"What are you saying? You said you had new information about Milla. What does that have to do with Seedlings?" Sarah asked, her voice rising in pitch.

"Sarah, sweetie," Ellen said.

"No," Sarah said, shaking off her aunt's comfort. "Are you saying you think Valerie killed Milla? Because that's the craziest thing I've ever heard. Valerie is the most amazing woman. She's been like a mother to me."

Ellen bristled ever so slightly.

Jeffers had told me Lindsey and her team had been doing some digging into Seedlings and had interviewed several parents who had had their children via one of Valerie's surrogates. All the clients had said glowing things about the experience and about Valerie herself, but they had also all said they had not been present for the birth of their children. Several had echoed Margo's story of it having been a fast labour and arriving just after the birth, while others had said there were complications during delivery that had required them to step out of the delivery room. One couple mentioned their surrogate had miscarried several months into the pregnancy.

If Milla had been one of Valerie's pregnant mothers, this is, undoubtedly, what the hopeful parents of her baby would have been told.

"Sarah," Jeffers said, "like I said, we are in the very early stages of investigation here, but, yes, at the moment, we are looking into Valerie and Seedlings."

"I still don't see how Milla fits into all of this," Rodney said.

"I had a chat with Cameron today."

"What do you mean?" Sarah asked.

"We can connect Cameron to a number of women who've gone missing over the last ten years."

"What?"

"I'm so sorry, Sarah," I said.

"You're wrong."

"We've also uncovered some unsettling things about his mother's business, and we think the two might be connected."

"No!"

"And you think Milla is one of these women?" Ellen asked. "But how is that even possible? Milla disappeared before Sarah even met Cameron."

Sarah looked directly at me, her eyes imploring me not to divulge that Sarah had taken her sister to Cameron's house four years ago.

"Mr. and Mrs. Koepper, Sarah," Jeffers said, "I know how distressing this news is and—"

"No, you don't," Sarah said. "You couldn't possibly. And, frankly, I don't understand how you can sit there and say something so outrageous. I think I know my fiancé."

"Sarah," I said, "we knew this would be upsetting for you all and, yes, it is unfathomable and yes, I hope we're wrong. But if we're not, you could be in danger."

"You think Cameron would hurt me?"

"We don't know," I said.

"I want you to go now."

"Sarah!" Rodney exclaimed.

"I'm sorry, Uncle Rod, but I can't listen to these ridiculous accusations about people I love, people who are my family. I won't."

"Sarah, they're just—"

"Don't tell me you believe what they're saying?" Sarah asked, her voice cracking.

"I—"

"Cameron and Valerie have had dinner in this house. Cameron helped you lay the driveway. He's laughed at every single one of your jokes. He's carried in how many bags of groceries, Aunt Ellen?"

"Dear, it—"

"They have been nothing but kind to you," she managed before breaking down completely.

Ellen held her niece tightly while she sobbed.

"We're so sorry," I said, getting up to leave.

Rodney stood to walk us out.

"This can't be happening," I heard Sarah mumble into Ellen's shoulder. "How could he do this? How? How could I not have seen?"

"Shhh," Ellen cooed, rocking Sarah gently.

"So, what now?" Paul asked me later that evening over drinks in his backyard.

The evening had cooled to a tolerable, almost pleasant, temperature. Moustache was sitting under the patio table chewing on his monthly tartar buster bone, looking up every so often to make sure there were no uninvited guests of the feline variety.

I shook my head. "I don't know. Jeffers said Lindsey and Crayne are trying to dig up as much as they can about Seedlings, but it hasn't been easy. It seems Valerie has been very good at presenting a legitimate business. Her employees seem devoted to her. Even the lawyers who have brokered the surrogacies appear to be above board."

"I still don't see how the missing women fit in. Or even could fit in. I know you said some of these women, like Milla, were runaways and an opportunity like this could be perceived as better than the alternative. But not all the women were runaways. How do you get them to present as if everything is okay in front of prospective parents?"

"Jeffers made that point."

"It doesn't make any sense."

"To me either."

"I mean, look at these testimonials," Paul said, flipping open one of the brochures Valerie had given us. "These are glowing words."

"Well, maybe they're fake," I said.

"What? The testimonials or the women?"

He picked up our glasses and carried them inside to refill them. Moustache jumped up to follow but saw that I remained sitting. Realizing there wasn't any immediate threat, he replopped himself under the table and resumed chewing.

I thought of Sarah's picture and the name Shona Murphy and wondered how many other stolen images Valerie had attributed false names and endorsements to. I had no idea how one might go about faking a surrogacy, but Paul's question about whether the testimonials or the women were fake ran on a loop in my mind and I began wondering what really might be possible.

I picked up my phone to run the notion past Jeffers. It rang in my hand. A number I didn't recognize.

"Hello?"

"Ms. James?"

"Yes."

"It's Sarah Ward."

Her voice was shaky although not as fraught as it had been when Jeffers and I left her in the arms of her aunt.

Paul returned with the drinks and a plate of crackers and cheese that immediately began to sweat. Moustache abandoned his bone to examine the plate. I gestured to the phone and put a finger to my lips.

"I talked to Cameron after you left. He told me about going to the police station and the questions he was asked. About all those women. He said he had nothing to do with them going missing. I asked him about Milla and he—"

She broke down crying.

I looked at Paul and mouthed Sarah Ward's name.

He raised his eyebrows and motioned to put the phone on speaker.

I knew I shouldn't and, if I did, I should tell Sarah someone else was listening. But I waved off both rules and hit the button, choosing to believe Paul's take on what she said was more important than respecting her privacy.

Her sobs filled the air, causing Moustache to cock his head and Paul to grimace.

"He swore to me he has nothing to do with what the police are saying," she said when she was able to get control over her emotions.

"And he may very well be telling the truth," I said. "Like my partner said at your house, there is still so much we don't know yet."

"I don't know what to believe," she said, giving way to tears again.

"In my experience," I said, gently, "it's best to listen to what your heart and your gut are telling you."

Sarah trusted me enough to call. I had already breached that trust by allowing Paul to listen in on our exchange, so I thought I at least owed it to her to be as honest as possible in my response.

"I love him," she said.

"Sarah," I said, "there are women who have been missing for a long time. Like Milla. We just want to find out what happened to them. We're exploring every angle. Just like we promised you and your family."

"I know." She took a deep, audible breath and when she spoke next, she spoke with resolve. "That's not the only reason I called. I went over to see Valerie. You know, about using my picture?"

"What did she say?"

"I didn't get a chance to speak with her. But I found something. Something I think you need to see."

Chapter 24

"She didn't say what it was?" Jeffers asked.

I had called him as soon as I hung up with Sarah.

"No. She just asked if we could meet her tomorrow. I have a window between my matinee and a friend's bachelorette party, so I told her anytime between five and seven would work. Is that good for you?"

"That should be fine."

"Great. I'll text Sarah and make sure that's okay with her and I'll confirm with you."

"Did she say where?"

"Seedlings. I can meet you there."

"Sounds good."

"Anything new on your end?"

"Keesha Rodrigues' phone records finally came in. I have no idea what took so long."

"And?"

"Nothing helpful. There's the call she made to her mother on the evening she disappeared and the call to

Kieran's clinic later that night. A few incoming calls on her machine from her mother's landline and Kieran but otherwise nothing else. The phone was either turned off or destroyed because the records end there."

"Damn."

"Yup. Crayne's got his team working on a bunch of stuff. I met with Morris earlier about sorting through the missing persons files to see which might fit this case. Going to be a long night."

"Well, I won't keep you. But before I let you go, try this on."

I went on to explain the fake surrogacy theory.

"So, you think there are women posing as surrogates who aren't actually pregnant?"

"I'm just wondering. It's an interesting possibility. I mean, I don't know how it would all work with the physical exams and everything, but it would explain why no parents we contacted had been present at the birth of their child."

My idea was met with silence.

Finally, Jeffers said, "Let me give it some thought. Run it by Morris and Crayne." I heard voices in Jeffers' background. "Samuel, I gotta go. Let me know what you set up with Sarah."

"Will do."

"It would be quite the scheme," Paul said after I'd put the phone down.

"Could something like that even be possible? Medically?"

"I guess it would if you have an ethically compromised medical staff on hand to treat the real pregnancies. As far as the other stuff, to me it seems like a technological issue."

"How do you mean?"

"Well, they'd have to fake the ultrasounds somehow. Especially if the parents are present. I don't know how you'd do that."

"*You* might not know how but somebody might. Right? Like hackers? Or tech whizzes?"

"Or cyberpunks?"

"Go ahead, make fun. But you know what I mean."

"I do," he said, laughing. "And I suppose anything is possible in this day and age."

"Hmmm," I said, contemplating the prospect and the wilted cheese plate.

"I should bring that inside," Paul said, following my gaze.

"I'll be in in a minute," I said.

Paul leaned over and kissed me before ferrying the cheese away to safety. Moustache followed him to the door then turned around and climbed up onto the seat next to me, laying his head in my lap with a satisfied snort.

The sky was clear and the stars were out in full force and, although the cheese had been sweating, it was the first time I hadn't been in ages. I wanted to enjoy the relative cool and the quiet, Moustache's soft breathing, and the lingering kiss on my lips.

"Where are you?" I asked Jeffers over the phone.

I was a few minutes late for our meeting with Sarah and expected Jeffers to be waiting.

"I'm not going to be able to make it. Can you handle meeting Sarah alone?"

"Of course. What's going on?"

"Milla's tox screen finally came in. You're not going to believe it. There were traces of poppy in her system."

"What?"

"Kieran lied to us. I'm just heading into his clinic."

"You're right, I don't believe it. Wow."

"Yeah. Bastard played us. Look, give me a call when you're finished with Sarah. I doubt I'll be finished here in time to meet you."

"No worries. I'll take care of it," I said, slightly dazed at Jeffers' revelation.

I checked my watch, hoping I wouldn't be long. Adam had planned a bridal shower/bachelorette party with a Kardashian theme. Fortunately, I didn't have a show until the following evening, which would give me the day to recuperate.

"Ms. James."

I turned to find Sarah walking toward me.

"You're alone?"

"Yes," I stammered, still processing the news about Kieran. "I'm afraid my partner had something urgent come up. I hope that's okay."

She nodded. "Oops, sorry," she said, pulling her phone out of the back pocket and thumbing a quick text. "My uncle keeps texting. I meant to turn this off."

"No need. I know this must be an anxious time for all of you."

"Yeah. Thank you for coming," she said, putting the phone away. "I wasn't sure if I should call you but…"

'I'm glad you did," I said, offering a warm smile that I hoped was reassuring.

"I guess I could have explained over the phone. It might be nothing, but Uncle Rod insisted so…"

"It was no trouble to come."

"Okay, good. It's … we have to go in through the back."

"Lead the way."

I followed Sarah as she set off along the side of the building.

"I don't want Valerie to see us," she said over her shoulder.

She held a screen door open for me and I stepped into the kitchen.

"I never come in here," she said. "But yesterday, when I was looking for Valerie, I heard voices back here and I thought maybe she was meeting with the cook."

I looked around the room. Nothing seemed odd or out of place.

"Is this what you wanted to show me?"

Sarah shook her head and led me into the pantry. "When I came in yesterday, that rack was swung open," she said, indicating a shelved section that held, among other things, various ingredients in Mason jars, club size containers of spices, and bags of rice.

My phone buzzed. I ignored it.

"What's behind it?"

"A doorway. I saw Valerie come out of it talking to a man in a white coat. I hid behind the dishwasher. She didn't see me. They mentioned something about Braxton Hicks."

"That's false labour," I said.

"I know. I remember my mom having that when she was pregnant with Milla."

There was a noise in the hallway outside, and Sarah led me deeper into the pantry, out of sight should anyone look into the kitchen.

My phone buzzed again.

"I didn't go down there, but I was thinking about what you said about those missing women and … Milla and…"

She started to cry.

"It's okay," I said, reaching out my hand and squeezing her shoulder.

She nodded and wiped her eyes. "It's probably nothing. Maybe just storage. But…"

"Well, why don't we go take a look so we know for sure."

Her eyes widened, fearful, but she swung the shelving unit to the side and revealed a doorway with a ramp leading downward. It was dimly lit. Sarah pulled out her phone and turned on the flashlight feature.

My phone buzzed a third time. I looked at the screen. It was Jeffers.

I rejected the call and set my phone to silent. I knew Sarah and I were on borrowed time and that someone could discover us at any moment. Whatever Jeffers needed to tell me about Kieran could wait.

The ramp led down to a hallway that was barely wide enough to accommodate the two of us walking side by side. The walls were stone, cold and damp, and the ground continued in an almost imperceptible decline.

We reached the end of the hallway and made a sharp right turn into another similar corridor.

"It's like a maze," Sarah said.

I heard footsteps behind us and turned to see Cameron Monroe approaching. His frame nearly filled the narrow hallway.

"Cameron," Sarah said, her voice wavering.

"What are you doing down here?" he asked.

"I…"

"Who are you?" he asked me.

"I'm Bella James. I work with the police. I've been working on Sarah's sister's case."

"Cameron, we—" Sarah started.

"You guys shouldn't be down here."

I looked to Sarah, who was standing a few steps behind me, leaving me as the monkey in the middle.

"It's okay," I said to her.

She nodded and smiled thankfully.

I felt a prick in my neck and twisted back around to see Cameron standing right next to me holding a syringe.

"What did you do?" I slurred, the words fumbling over themselves on their way out of my mouth.

Cameron didn't answer. He just stared and waited for my vision to blur and my knees to buckle.

I fell to the ground. I felt boneless. My mouth was moving, making incoherent sounds. My eyes closed as if the lids had been glued together. A rush of euphoria flooded my brain and, in an instant, a pleasure so intense filled my entire being that my will to fight vanished. I allowed my head to loll to one side and I relaxed into the warm embrace of unconsciousness.

Chapter 25

"Where's the other cop?"

"He got called away on something. I texted you."

The voices were muddled by the fog in my brain, but I could still make out what they were saying.

I was being carried. My body felt heavy, resistant to even the thought of movement. I managed a thin slit between my eyelids and saw that we were approaching a metal door.

I guessed I'd only been out for a few seconds, although I didn't think my current state resembled anything close to consciousness. I closed my eyes and listened, not wanting to give any indication that I was hearing their conversation.

"He's going to come looking for her, you know."

"I'll tell him she met with me like I asked her to, and then she left when we were done. Why would I know where she'd be going after that?"

"And what will you tell him about why you wanted to meet her?"

"Cameron, jeez, I don't know, okay. Can we just deal with her first and figure out the rest later?"

"I'm just saying."

I heard the beeps of a code being punched in on a keypad and a click as the door opened.

We moved forward a few steps before stopping again in front of another steel door.

"Maybe you should wait here for him to show up and deal with him like you were supposed to."

"Don't turn this around on me," Cameron said. "I was ready. It's not my fault he didn't come."

"I know. I'm sorry. I'm just…"

"Babe, it's okay. We'll figure it out."

My last ounce of lucidity dissolved and I was enveloped in oblivion once again.

When I woke up, a woman came immediately to my side.

"Drink this," she said. "The sedative causes severe dehydration. It could hurt your baby."

"I'm not … I'm not … pregnant," I said, summoning the strength to sit up.

I was in a room that reminded me of a hospital ward from a WWII movie. Two rows of beds lined the walls with an aisle between.

"What are you doing here, then?" The woman asked. "They only bring pregnant women here."

"I work with the police," I said, my head pounding.

The woman's eyes widened. "Well, you should drink this anyway," she said, raising a plastic cup to my lips and helping a yogurty liquid into my mouth.

I could feel my strength returning.

"So, are you undercover or something?" she whispered. "Are you here to save us?"

"I—"

The woman looked over her shoulder and motioned someone over with her hand. "She's with the police," she said when the other woman had joined us.

I looked up.

"Keesha Rodrigues," I said. "You're alive. Thank god."

I could see the slightest hint of pregnancy through Keesha's nightgown.

"Are you really with the police?" she asked.

I nodded. "I'm not a cop, but I work with them sometimes. We've been investigating Milla Ward's death and it led us … here. What is this place?"

"The baby factory," Keesha said.

Keesha would have given birth to her first baby approximately seven months after she went missing. To be pregnant again within six months was a quick turnaround. A baby factory, indeed.

"Finish this," the other woman said, placing the cup in my hands. "Trust me."

"What's your name?" I asked, taking another sip of the liquid.

"Morgan. Morgan Aymes."

Her name didn't ring a bell, but I hadn't been privy to all the records Jeffers and Lindsey had been cross-referencing.

There was so much I wanted to know. So many questions I wanted to ask. But as my mind cleared and my body started to feel like its normal self, I knew the first course of action was to get a hold of Jeffers. I reached for my phone.

"They took it," Morgan said. "Not that it would really matter if they let you keep it. It wouldn't work down here anyway."

"But Milla," I said, looking at Keesha. "She made a call from your phone."

Keesha nodded. "I had two phones on me when I was brought here. One was my mom's. I had picked it up from getting repaired. They took it thinking it was mine. They never bothered to check for another one."

"And by 'they' you mean Sarah and Cameron?"

"Yeah. When Milla saw that I had a phone, she came up with a plan to get Sarah to take her upstairs. She told me she had found a business card with her boyfriend's name on it. It had fallen out of Cameron's pocket one day and she had held on to it, waiting for a chance. Waiting for a miracle.

"When she was brought back down, she was heavily sedated—more so than usual. I was afraid she wouldn't come out of it. The phone was gone."

So, Kieran was the one supplying poppies to Cameron. Jeffers must have figured that out when he confronted Kieran at the clinic and tried to warn me. I kicked myself for having dismissed his calls.

"Does anyone know you're here?" Morgan asked, hopefully.

"My partner knows I was coming, but I overheard Sarah and Cameron concocting a plan to throw him off the scent."

Or take him out.

I didn't want to think of the latter. And I didn't have much time.

I looked around the room. There were six other women lying in beds. Two appeared to be sleeping and the others sat under clouds of despondency.

I caught the eye of a blonde woman who I thought might be the same age as me and smiled. She held my gaze but didn't smile back.

These women were broken. Hopeless. Resigned.

I stood up on shaky legs and took a minute to steady my balance. Every step I took felt like I was walking on the deck of a ship in turbulent waters.

Outside the dormitory was a long hallway that led to a steel door with a round window. Standing on my toes I could see a space that I guessed served as an insemination, exam, and delivery room. Further along the corridor was another room.

"The kitchen," Morgan said.

"Well, not really," Keesha corrected. "It's where the food is delivered."

"Who brings it to you?"

"See that there," she said, pointing to a rectangular opening I judged to be about a foot high and a little more than that wide. "There's a conveyor belt in there. All our food comes down on that."

I peeked inside. There was no way a person could climb through.

"How do you get into the exam room?" I asked. There was no lock or handle on the door.

"One of the doctors or nurses lets us in."

"How often do they come?"

"They're in and out of here several times a day," Morgan explained.

"Do they have a code or a key?"

Morgan shook her head. "The door operates remotely."

"What do you mean?"

"I mean someone watches and opens the door when they're standing right in front of it." She jutted her chin at the corner of the hallway. "There are cameras everywhere."

My heart sank. If they were watching our every move, I had no hope of contacting Jeffers. Or escaping.

Thoughts of Moustache and Paul rolled together to form a knot in my stomach, and I buried my head in my hands.

I felt a comforting hand on my back and pushed back the tears that were threatening to come. These women had been through much more, had lost so much more. I would not cry in front of them. That wasn't what they needed. They needed me at Emma Samuel's best.

And I needed to think.

There had to be a way to let Jeffers, someone, anyone, know we were here. That this lair existed.

I looked through the window of the examination room again, searching for something we could use. I needed to get in there.

"Can they hear us?" I asked.

Both Morgan and Keesha shrugged.

I lowered my voice just in case. "Okay, listen very carefully."

Chapter 26

It was close to ten minutes before help arrived. Whoever was watching was slow on the draw.

Keesha had done an exemplary job feigning pain and maintaining the ruse while we waited for the wizard behind the curtain to notice and send assistance. She was curled up on the floor moaning when the door finally hissed open.

The nurse rushed immediately to Keesha's side. She smelled like she'd just finished a cigarette.

"My, my, my, what do we have here?" the nurse said, bending over to assess Keesha's condition.

The concern on her face and in her voice was genuine. She might have had no qualms about keeping these women prisoner, but at least she seemed to care about their well-being.

"She was fine and then she just doubled over," I said. I was sitting on the floor holding Keesha's hand.

"Probably just some routine cramping, but it's best we find out for sure," she said to Keesha. "Let's get up and into the exam room so I can take a look at what's going on."

She spoke with kindness and calming reassurance.

Morgan and I helped the nurse get Keesha to her feet. After a couple of seconds, the exam room door opened and we proceeded inside.

As per my instructions, Keesha maintained a hold on my hand, even when we finally got her settled onto the bed.

"Back to your room now," the nurse said to me.

Keesha moaned and tightened her grip.

"I think she wants me to stay," I said.

The nurse looked at me sharply, as if seeing me for the first time. "Who are you?"

"She's new,'" Morgan said from the doorway. "They brought her in today."

"Ah," said the nurse. "In that case, Morgan here can fill you in on the rules. The first one is that you girls aren't permitted in the exam room unless it's for a procedure."

"But she—"

"She is at extremely high risk given how quickly they impregnated her again after her first delivery," the nurse said, almost whispering. "And if she is going to get the help she needs, you will leave this room immediately or someone will come down and remove you. Do you understand?"

I understood perfectly well that my plan had failed.

I looked at Keesha and nodded. She reluctantly released my hand and I walked out to join Morgan in the hall.

"How can you do this?" I asked, turning back to the nurse. "You know these women are here against their will. You know what is being done to them. What has been done to them repeatedly. Women have died. And yet you come here day after day. How can you live with yourself?"

"Everyone has a price," she said, her eyes locked on mine. "Consider yourself lucky no one has figured out yours."

The door hissed shut.

Morgan took me by the hand and began to lead me back to the dormitory.

I felt something hard against my palm.

"It fell out of the nurse's pocket when she bent down to help Keesha," Morgan said, letting go of my hand and looking straight ahead so as not to draw attention. "I grabbed it when we were helping Keesha up. The nurse didn't notice it fall. She probably didn't realize it was in her pocket. They're not allowed to bring anything in."

"Why not?"

"One time, one of the doctors had his car keys in his pocket. Rhiannon got a hold of them and almost gouged his eyes out. Ever since then…"

"What happened to Rhiannon?"

"She's … I don't know what they did to her, but she's never been the same again."

I wrapped my fingers around the object and began my deduction.

A lighter. Not a fancy one, by any means. A cheap one you could pick up at the drugstore. I thought of the smell that had wafted in when the nurse arrived. She must have been outside smoking when the emergency call had been raised and had put the lighter in her pocket in her rush to get down here.

I caught Morgan's eye and she allowed herself a small smile. "Now we just have to find something to burn."

"I can help," said the blonde woman I had smiled at earlier. "Meet me in the bathroom."

Morgan had quietly and carefully spread the news of the lighter to the other women in the dormitory. I noticed she didn't mention it to two of the women and, when I asked her about it, she said that both were pretty much catatonic, their bodies barely more than incubators.

One had wild, orange hair, and I guessed she was Rhiannon. Or had been.

When Morgan mentioned the lighter to the blonde woman, it was like something inside her woke up.

"Pretend I'm giving you the tour," she said when I joined her in the bathroom.

There were two toilets and three showers, all of which had privacy doors. That surprised me given the amount of surveillance. There was also a large, communal sink with foot pedals.

The blonde woman led me to a cabinet at the far end of the room.

"Everything we need to start a fire is right here," she said, opening the cabinet's doors.

It was filled with bars of soap, bottles of shampoo, feminine hygiene products, lotions, and a myriad of other common toiletries.

"I don't understand," I said.

"We need tinder," she said, pointing to several boxes of maxi pads. "And an accelerant," she said, moving a jar of Vaseline from one shelf to another.

To anyone watching, it would look like one girl was showing the new girl where the necessities were stored rather than the pyrotechnics lesson it was turning out to be.

"Once we get the fire started, we can burn anything. The cardboard from all these boxes and the toilet paper rolls, the toilet paper, even our clothing."

"How do you know all this?" I asked.

"My dad. He used to take us camping a lot. Used to take a few of my mom's tampons with us. It used to really bug her, but she never stayed mad at him for long."

She spoke with a mixture of sadness and detachment.

"How long have you been here?" I asked.

"Long enough to have had five babies," she said, shutting the cupboard and walking over to a set of shelves next to the showers.

She showed me where clean towels and nighties were kept and where dirty ones were to be placed, all the while pointing out a vent in the wall and explaining that if we started a fire inside it, the flames and smoke would rise to the main floor. If we were lucky.

It seemed to be our only option. The steel door would curtail the spread of the fire if we started it anywhere else.

"Won't they see us? Stop us?"

"I don't think they watch us too closely at night. I'm not even sure anyone is here overnight. The times we've had an emergency, it's taken ages for someone to come." She held a nightie up against me as if gauging its size. "We should have plenty of time to get the fire started. What we really need is time for it to burn. That's the only way it will get attention."

She folded the nightie, picked up another, and went through the same pretense of judging its fit.

"After I leave, take a box of pads into the stall and pull a couple of them apart. What we need is the cotton. Don't stay too long. We don't want them to get curious. Leave the box in there. I'll come back in a little while and coat the cotton with Vaseline and shape it into balls. Once I've made a few, you guys will know what to do. We'll have to work one at a time."

"Okay," I said, staring at her in amazement.

"My dad was also the Deputy Fire Chief at the Niagara Falls Fire Department," she said, handing me a nightgown I had no intention of putting on. "I'm Sasha, by the way."

"Bella."

She nodded and left.

Over the next few hours and carefully spaced out visits to the bathroom, we had successfully transformed the box of pads into an impressive collection of fire starters. Based on the time I had arrived for my meeting with Sarah, I guessed it to be around nine p.m. There was no way of telling time in the bowels of the building.

There was also no way of knowing what Cameron and Sarah might have done to Jeffers.

Keesha returned from a shift in the bathroom, and I went over to join her on her bed. "Do you mind if I ask you a few questions?"

"Not at all," she said.

"I guess the obvious one is how you ended up here."

"Cameron brought me."

"Willingly?"

"I don't know how much you know, but I was pregnant and I didn't want to keep it. He said his mother ran this clinic and could help me. So, yeah, I came willingly. Little did I know."

"You and Cameron were friends?"

"Not really. He used to pick up deliveries at the place I worked, and we'd chat sometimes. Have you met him?"

"Not really. Only over the phone and in the hallway before he drugged me."

"But you would have heard it. His way of speaking. It's so calming, almost entrancing. I never thought about it in the moment but, after talking to him, I'd be shocked by how much I'd divulged."

I smiled as I recollected my own first impressions of Cameron when he'd called Jeffers after our visit to Kelly's.

"Anyway," Keesha continued, "one day, I told him about the pregnancy and how I wanted to have an abortion, and he said his mother would be able to get me in right away, so I drove straight to the clinic after work. He and his mom set me up in one of the rooms upstairs and gave me a sedative for the procedure. But when I woke up, I was still pregnant, and I was here in this room. Been here ever since."

I wondered if something similar had happened to Bernadelle. A seemingly random act of kindness that was laced with ulterior motives.

"What happened to your baby?" I asked.

She shrugged. "It was born and they took it. I really have no idea. I don't even know if it was a boy or a girl."

The overhead lights clicked off, plunging the dormitory into darkness.

It was a sign for us to go to sleep. It was also the moment we'd been waiting for.

Our cue to begin.

Sasha slipped out of her bed and padded into the bathroom. Moments later she returned and handed each woman a wet face cloth.

"This might not work," I said to Keesha. "There's a very good chance no one will come and we'll all die tonight."

Whether by smoke inhalation, burning, or a fate Cameron or Sarah would undoubtedly impose.

"We're all going to die here anyway," she said. "No one leaves here alive. Light it up."

A slow, quiet chant of "light it up" filled the room.

I looked to Sasha. "Is everything ready?" I asked.

"Just waiting on the flame."

"Okay. Here we go," I said to the women, interrupting their chant. "You know what to do."

The women got out of their beds and gathered in the small kitchen. The distance wouldn't save them if fire or smoke engulfed the area, but it would be helpful to get as far away from the fire while waiting for help to arrive. Keesha and Morgan helped the two unresponsive women out of bed. I was certain they had no idea what was happening.

I joined Sasha in the bathroom.

Once we secured wet towels around our mouths and noses, Sasha retrieved our stash of kindling from the toilet stall and deftly removed the vent cover, placing a few of the Vaseline-saturated balls inside.

I reached into my pocket for the lighter and felt the wedding band I had put there in case I ran into Valerie while at Seedlings to meet Sarah.

Tears sprang to my eyes and I stifled a sob.

I handed the lighter to Sasha, slipped the ring onto my finger, and stood at the ready to hand her the things we had gathered to burn.

Sasha held the lighter over one of the cotton balls and her eyes met mine.

"You heard the ladies. Light it up."

We knew within seconds that the air flow was working for us. The first fire starter had caught quickly, and we both breathed a sigh of relief as the smoke began to rise in the vent. After adding all the boxes and toilet paper rolls, we managed an impressive blaze.

The air was thick with a dark haze and the towel covering Sasha's face was showing signs of blackening. Tears poured from our eyes, and we squeezed them shut against the sting.

"Hand me the sheets," Sasha said, positioning herself even lower to the ground.

I passed them over and followed her lead by dropping to my belly.

She worked the sheets in carefully so as not to smother the fire.

"Now go join the others," she said.

"I'm not leaving you here."

We were speaking louder now as the sound of the fire increased.

"There's nothing left for you to do. I'm going to put in these last couple of sheets and then I'll come."

I said nothing and stayed where I was.

"Go, Bella."

I coughed and nodded. "If you're not out in five minutes, I'm coming back."

"Go," she said, looking into the vent. "Go now."

I pulled myself up to my hands and knees and crawled in the direction of the dormitory. I had just turned the corner when I heard an explosion and a rush of flame burst into the sleeping quarters. I dove under the closest bed and watched as the fire began to work its way through the mattresses and bedding on the other side of the room.

"Sasha!" I yelled.

No answer.

I yelled again.

I shimmied out from under the bed and, clutching my towel to my face, inched back into the bathroom.

I called Sasha's name again, but the sound was muffled by the smoke and the towel and the burning sensation in my lungs.

I crawled deeper into the room, tears obscuring my vision for the few seconds at a time that I was able to keep my eyes open.

Finally, I saw a shape in one of the toilet stalls.

It looked as if Sasha had been thrown back in the blast. She wasn't moving and looked to have suffered a few burns, but the shelter of the stall had protected her from severe injury.

I didn't know if she was alive, and I didn't have time to check.

I unwrapped the towel from my face and fashioned a kind of sling under her arms. And then with everything I had, I pulled.

Through the bathroom, into the dormitory, under the blanket of smoke that had filled the bedroom area while the fire wreaked its havoc, I pulled until I fell gasping and spent into the hallway where the other women waited, huddled together, as far away from the fire's path as they could get.

Keesha was on me at once. Pulling me out of harm's way and into the hallway's depth. Morgan saw to Sasha and immediately began administering CPR when she had arrived at a safe distance.

For the moment, the hallway remained untouched by the flames, although I could feel the air thickening and the wall that separated us from the sleeping area getting warmer.

I tried to speak but was choked by a mouthful of hot air that brought me to my knees in a fit of coughing before collapsing onto the ground that was still, somehow, miraculously cool. I curled into the comfort of the floor, a headache throbbing against the inside of my skull. Rhythmic and unrelenting, the beating became so intense that it was all I could hear as it clobbered me from the inside.

The women started screaming. Crying. Hugging each other.

I brought my hands to my ears and rolled myself into a tighter ball, trying to drown out the sound.

The screaming, the pounding.

I felt someone's hands on me. Shaking me. I opened my eyes to find Keesha kneeling in front of me. Her mouth was moving, but I couldn't make out what she was saying. The constant banging inside my head overpowered the sound of her voice.

The constant banging overpowered everything.

Chapter 27

And then it stopped.

The women fell silent and held their collective breath. Keesha looked toward the steel door of our prison, and I followed her gaze.

The door swung open.

There were lights. Voices. I felt myself being picked up and carried, for the second time that day, through the underground labyrinth.

There was yelling and a rush of activity, and I was pressed against a wall as bodies moved past me. Gradually, the air got lighter, clearer, and I choked on the cleanliness of it.

I felt a rush of fresh air as we burst outside into a sea of flashing red and blue.

I was handed off to another set of arms, lowered onto a gurney, and a mask was placed over my face. My lungs thirstily drank in the oxygen.

Two faces hovered over me asking questions.

"Let me through," I heard someone yell, and a moment later Jeffers was at my side.

One of the paramedics stepped between us. "Sir, I'm going to need you to—"

"It's Detective, and this is my partner. I'm not going anywhere."

"I'm okay," I managed to say before coughing took hold.

"Ma'am, you need to keep your mask on," the paramedic said. "And, Detective, I know you're concerned about your partner, but she has suffered severe smoke inhalation and we need to treat her. So, with all due respect, I'm going to ask you to step aside and let us do our work."

"Is she going to be all right?" Jeffers asked the paramedic.

"As long as we get in there before her airway swells."

Jeffers stepped aside and both paramedics swooped in.

"I'll call Paul and tell him to meet us at the hospital," Jeffers said.

I nodded.

"Ma'am, we're going to hook you up to an IV so we can give you some medication, all right?"

I nodded again.

"You're going to lose consciousness," the paramedic explained, "and then we're going to put a tube down your throat. It's going to help you breathe, and it's going to give us a chance to assess the damage, okay?"

"Bella, you're going to be fine, do you hear me?" Jeffers said.

I felt a prick in my right arm, heard the ambulance doors close, and when I opened my eyes, I was in the hospital with curtains drawn around my bed.

"She's awake." I heard Paul's voice before I saw him. "Don't try to talk," he said to me. "You've still got the breathing tube in."

He was sitting in a chair on one side of the bed. Jeffers was pacing the six feet of floor on the other. He dragged a second chair over and smiled.

"The doctor said your x-ray didn't show any damage to the lungs, and your bloodwork came back clean. You might have some trouble breathing for a little while, and you should get lots of rest, but you're going to be fine."

I nodded.

He looked relieved.

"Miss James," a nurse said, pulling the curtain aside and approaching my bedside. "You feeling okay? Just nod or shake your head."

I thought it was an odd question. I was clearly not okay, but I certainly felt better than I had when I was brought to the ambulance, so I nodded.

"Good. I'm going to take the breathing tube out now. I want you to take a deep breath and, on my say, I want you to cough. The more you cough, the easier it will be, okay?"

I nodded.

Paul brought my hand to his lips, and after a few of the most unpleasant seconds of my life, the tube was out.

"How—"

"Try not to speak," the nurse said. "You inhaled a lot of smoke. You need to rest. I'll let the doctor know you're awake."

I tried to ask Jeffers how he found us, but what came out of my mouth were a jumble of raspy sounds that only resembled a few of the words I had wanted to say. Luckily, he got the gist.

"I tried to call you. Warn you about Sarah and Cameron. But you didn't answer. Then I got a text from you asking me to meet you at Seedlings."

I shook my head.

"I know it wasn't from you. Cameron tried to jump me in the parking lot. Idiot. He may be big, but I learned a few tricks when I worked at BEU."

I smiled. Jeffers was slightly built, and I had always found it funny that he'd once worked with the Biker Enforcement Unit.

"With him in custody for assaulting a police officer, I stopped by the Koepper house to ask Sarah about your meeting. She said you'd come and gone. Whichever of them was to have disposed of your car hadn't gotten around to it yet, so I knew she was lying. Your car's still in the lot, by the way."

"Good," I croaked.

"I'll spare you the full play-by-play," he said. "Basically, when the call came in about the fire, I squeezed Cameron for info. He finally spilled about the basement lock-up."

"That's one point in his favour, I guess," Paul said.

"He needs all the help he can get."

"The fire idea was risky."

"I know," I said.

"If Cameron hadn't talked…"

"I know."

Paul tightened his grip on my hand and the three of us sat in silence for a few moments.

"Kieran?" I managed.

"Not involved."

I raised my eyebrows in surprise and felt a slight twinge. I immediately brought my hand to my forehead to check if they were still there.

"You might need a bit of make-up on the left one," Paul said, gently.

I grunted and looked back to Jeffers.

"Did you know there are more than seventy kinds of poppies? And not only that. There's a whole whack of those herbalists—or whatever they're called—all over the world. They're a real thing!"

Paul laughed and I rolled my eyes.

"Anyway, poppies grown legally can be used as anesthetic. Sarah and Cameron have bought from Kieran's clinic a couple of times. Kieran had no idea Sarah was Milla's sister. Steven managed to track down some of their other suppliers as well. My guess is they wanted to give the women a natural sedative so as not to harm the babies and wanted to spread out their buying to draw less attention to themselves. I brought Kieran in for questioning but everything checks out. He was devastated to learn the part his plants played in Milla's captivity."

"Detective," the nurse said, poking her head around the curtain, "someone's asking for you."

"I should let you get some rest anyway. Give you two some time."

I nodded and smiled.

"Thanks, man," Paul said, shaking Jeffers' hand.

He pulled aside the curtain but stopped and looked back to me. Whatever biker bravado he had mustered when facing Cameron was nowhere to be found. In that moment, he was not a cop. Just a friend filled with worry and wracked with guilt.

"I should never have let you go alone," he said, his voice breaking slightly.

"You couldn't have stopped me," I said with rather a lot of difficulty.

"I know," he said.

"I'm going to be fine."

"You better."

I nodded and he left.

"Sasha?"

"Shhh," said the nurse.

"Is she…" I stumbled over what word to finish the sentence with.

"Everyone's fine. You're all in the ward here together," the nurse said with a smile before glancing at Paul and exiting the way Jeffers had.

"I'll go see what I can find out," Paul said after she left.

I nodded but didn't let go of his hand.

He looked at me through worried eyes and squeezed my hand tighter. In doing so, he noticed the wedding band I had slipped onto my finger and started to laugh.

Embarrassed, I tried to utter some explanation, but he silenced me by holding up his own left hand, similarly adorned.

"I thought they might not let me see you because I'm not family so … Besides, I've kind of gotten used to wearing it."

"Me too."

"I'll be right back," he said, kissing my forehead and then my lips.

This time I let him go.

He pulled the drape that separated me from the next bed and froze.

"What's the matter?" I croaked.

He didn't move.

"Honey?"

His knees buckled, and he stumbled to the chair next to my bed. His face was ashen.

I pressed the call button for the nurse as I struggled to free myself from IV tubes and blankets.

"Paul, what is it?"

He moved his mouth wordlessly, his face pale and distressed.

I called for the nurse as loudly as I could manage and hammered on the call button.

A different nurse came running in, her eyes widening as she caught sight of the disarray I had produced.

"It's not me," I said. "It's my … husband. He's not well."

"Sir," she said, moving to Paul's side. "Sir, can you tell me what's wrong?"

"He opened that curtain," I said, "and his legs just gave out."

"Sir?" The nurse said, taking his wrist in her hands and checking his pulse.

"Who's over there? The other nurse said all of us from the fire were here together. Is it Sasha? Is she dead?"

"I'm afraid we haven't been able to identify the woman next door," the nurse said, pulling a pen light from her pocket and shining it in Paul's eyes.

He squinted and turned away from the glare. "Her name is Laura."

Chapter 28

"Laura? As in his former girlfriend Laura?"

"Fiancée, yes. That's why they never found her body."

Jeffers whistled.

I had been discharged from the hospital in the morning. Paul had picked me up and ferried me to the police station and had returned to check on Laura's condition. Other than some mild smoke inhalation, she hadn't been injured in the fire, but her years in captivity on top of the already fragile mental state Paul had told me about had not been kind.

Morgan told me that in all her time there, Laura had given birth to three babies but had never spoken, and that the other women had taken it upon themselves to feed and bathe her.

"How is he doing?" Jeffers asked.

"He's a mess. For four years he thought she was dead. He believed her suicide note. It wasn't her first attempt, and so he honoured her wish for him to not look for her. He blames himself entirely for this."

"He wouldn't have found her."

"I know that, and you know that. There's probably even a part of him that knows that, but, for the moment, none of it matters."

"And how are you doing?"

"I don't know," I said. "There's so much to process."

"What about physically?"

"Talking still hurts a bit, and it's hard taking a deep breath, but it's getting easier."

I had a performance that evening and was waiting until absolutely necessary to call my stage manager and my understudy. I wasn't delusional. I knew what it took to vocally project to the back row of the audience and, while I was hopeful the day would afford me the rest I needed, I was doubtful it would be enough.

"Are you sure you're up for this?"

"Absolutely."

We started a slow walk to the interrogation rooms.

A team had arrested Valerie and Sarah the night before, and additional charges had been laid against Cameron. Valerie and Cameron had lawyered up immediately. Jeffers told me that Valerie had been quick to claim full responsibility in an attempt to protect her son.

"She said she would go with Cameron when he made deliveries to the food banks, looking for pregnant women too down on their luck to question her offer of natal care. She encountered Angela Hansen in a bathroom during one of her scouting missions. Said the poor woman was so far gone, she was able to simply whisk her into the van. She'd get them back to Seedlings, examine them, and, if the pregnancy was healthy, move them downstairs. Sell the babies when they were born and then use the women as surrogates, knowing they'd be able to sustain future pregnancies."

"That's disgusting."

"The last woman taken was Keesha. Her baby would have been sold months ago. That's why there's been no recent activity from any of the people we've been watching on the dark web."

"Of course. All the current pregnancies are spoken for."

"But it's one step closer to the baby ring. It's clear Valerie is one of their suppliers. We just have to keep her talking. And, in the meantime, Steven's going through her computer."

"My god, has someone been in touch with the prospective parents?" I asked, thinking of all the couples waiting to welcome home their new sons and daughters.

"Lindsey's team is taking care of that."

I shuddered at the thought of being on the receiving end of a call like that. I wondered how Margo would react when she found out the circumstances surrounding Nora's birth.

"There's also the question of the babies who were sold. Angela Hansen's baby is out there somewhere. And Bernadelle's. Their families are going to want to find them. This whole thing is going to take ages to sort out."

I thought of Angela's husband and Mirsad, Bernadelle's boyfriend. These babies, children now, were all they had left of the women they loved.

"Oh, and Valerie tried to tell me Cameron had no idea what she was doing. She said she told him she was just being kind, offering care to women who might not be receiving it elsewhere. She said he never saw the women from the shelters after they were brought into the exam rooms. As far as he knew, they had the exam and left."

"Well, we know that's nowhere even close to true."

Although I hadn't heard every woman's story, I guessed many of them would have experienced something along the lines of Keesha's version of events, which saw Cameron directly involved in her abduction. And, according to Keesha and Morgan, Cameron and Sarah were the ones giving all the orders. And the punishments when one of them misbehaved.

"Did she say how she managed the surrogacies with the would-be parents?" I asked.

"Hired women who pretended to be pregnant and fitted them with high-end prosthetic bellies. They had all different kinds to represent the various stages of pregnancy. I had a look at one and couldn't believe how real it looked."

"And these were the women the parents met with?"

"Yup."

"Sarah."

Jeffers nodded. "AKA Shona Murphy. We're in the process of tracking down some of the others."

"Did any of the parents mention kicking? I mean, the parents must have wanted to feel the baby moving around. That wouldn't have been possible. How did they get around that?"

"I asked them that exact question. I always had my hands on Aria when she was pregnant. One of the mothers said the baby was never active when they visited, but the surrogate assured her it kicked plenty. She'd been disappointed but understood you couldn't control something like that."

"And what about the exams?"

"The ultrasound machines in the exam rooms upstairs at Seedlings were linked to one in the basement. They'd conduct an ultrasound on the real pregnant woman downstairs and would go through the motions upstairs with the fake surrogate at the same time. The parents got to see real visuals of their baby."

"Wow."

"Want to hear about the deliveries?" Jeffers asked.

"I'm not sure."

"The woman would give birth in the basement, and a nurse would send the baby to the room upstairs on some sort of conveyor belt."

"The kitchen," I said.

"What?"

"It's how the women got their meals."

Jeffers shook his head. "I hate to think what more I'm going to learn when I get a chance to talk to them."

"What about Cameron?"

"He denied everything until he couldn't. Finally corroborated his mother's story about her accompanying him on deliveries to soup kitchens to look for pregnant women. He also confessed to luring women to the clinic with promises of quick, safe abortions, drugging them when they got there, and adding them to his collection."

"Like Keesha and Bernadelle."

"Yeah. And others, like Sasha. I hear it was pretty touch and go with her for a while but she's pulled through."

"Yes. There was a lot of damage to her lungs and a fracture from the blast but she's going to be fine, thank goodness. She was the real hero. If it weren't for her, we never would have gotten out of there."

I began coughing with the exertion and had to stop walking to bring it under control.

"Jesus, Bella, you sound terrible. Why don't you go home? We're going to record the interview. I can bring it by later."

Sarah hadn't requested a lawyer when she was brought in, and Jeffers had taken a great risk holding off interviewing her until the morning so I'd be able to watch through a two-way mirror.

I shook my head and resumed walking.

When I finally had my breath, I asked, "Did Valerie or Cameron say why they did it?"

"For Valerie, it was money. Her going rate for one pregnancy was well above the going rate of a typical surrogacy. She claimed the difference in cost was because of the convenience of having all the medical procedures done on site. She paid the fake surrogates an attractive amount, and Arnold Reymer referred couples to her for a fee that paid for his silence more than anything. She wasn't paying the women who were actually pregnant, which is the biggest cost in surrogacy, so after operating costs and lawyer fees, she walked away with a hefty sum."

"What about the doctors and nurses?"

"We haven't had a chance to speak with them yet."

I thought about what the nurse had said to me about everyone having a price, and I imagined there was some kind of blackmail at play.

"From what I've been able to gather," Jeffers continued, "Valerie wasn't really involved in the actual handling of things once she procured the women. I got the feeling she didn't agree with Cameron's method of recruitment, but she needed him to do the dirty work, so she let him do his thing. I think she had no idea about a lot of what went on down there."

"And Cameron's motive?"

"Also money, to some degree. Valerie paid him well to manage the women, but he figured the more there were to manage, the bigger the payday, so he took what he called 'some initiative.' And I think there's an element of control there that he got off on. He said he was expected to go into the family business whether he wanted to or not. He said a lot of things that made me realize that, in his mind, Kelly's had indentured him. I think he was looking for something, anything, that he could be master of."

He stopped and opened the door in front of us.

I was stunned to find Rodney and Ellen already seated in the viewing room when I entered.

"We needed to be here," Rodney said, seeing my surprise. "We needed to hear for ourselves."

Ellen's eyes were red and puffy, and she clung to her husband's hand.

"I'm so sorry," I said, even though I knew it wasn't nearly enough.

"We heard what happened," Rodney said. "Are you…?"

"I'm fine," I said. "Thank you."

He smiled, sadly.

Sarah was sitting at a table on the other side of the glass. She looked small and nervous and seemed to shrink further still when Jeffers took his seat across from her.

Lindsey joined Jeffers a moment later while Crayne and Morris slipped into the room to watch with me and the Koeppers.

Crayne's eyes were sympathetic and kind when he looked at me, and he offered a small smile, but neither man said anything.

Lindsey turned on a video camera, officially stated the time and date, and identified the people in the room.

Sarah shifted in her chair.

I couldn't get a read on her. She didn't seem defiant or defensive. Or remorseful. If anything, she looked like she simply wanted to disappear.

"Sarah," Lindsey began, "I'd like you to tell me about your relationship with Valerie Kinsey."

"She's my boyfriend's mother," Sarah said, quietly.

"But you had a relationship with her prior to that, right?" Sarah pursed her lips and eventually nodded. "Tell me about that."

"Val was my mother's friend."

"Your mother also worked for Valerie, didn't she? Valerie used to pimp her out, isn't that right?"

"Sometimes. When we really needed money."

"You worked for Valerie too."

"Not … doing that. She doesn't do that anymore. And I would never…"

"What was your job, then?"

Sarah took a sip from the water glass in front of her. "I … was a pretend surrogate."

"And can you explain what that entailed?"

She sat for a moment, avoiding both Jeffers' and Lindsey's gazes. I didn't know if she was trying to figure out how to answer or if she was reconsidering her desire for representation. When she finally spoke, she reiterated much of what Valerie had told Jeffers about the "surrogacy" process.

"Where did you think the babies came from?"

"I didn't know."

"You never asked?"

Sarah shrugged.

"When did you first learn women were being kept in the basement?"

Sarah looked down and began playing with her fingers.

"Miss Ward, the women you kept in that cellar have all named you and your fiancé and Valerie as their captors. And Ms. Kinsey and Mr. Monroe have already confessed.

So, let me be clear—we don't need your testimony. What we're doing here is giving you the chance to share your side of the story."

Sarah remained silent. A pained expression formed on her face, and I wondered if it was just sinking in that she really had no way out of this.

"I'm going to ask you again," Lindsey said. "When did you first learn of the women in the basement?"

"Was it four years ago when you brought your sister to Cameron after she showed up at your aunt and uncle's house?" Jeffers asked.

I heard Ellen gasp next to me.

Sarah looked at the two-way mirror. There was no way she could have heard her aunt's exclamation, and I didn't know if she knew who was there listening, but she stared at the glass, eyes pleading. Her jaw began to tremble.

"Sarah," Jeffers said, allowing himself to sound more sympathetic than official. A tone opposite to Lindsey's. "You told my partner that Milla came to the house. Is that true?"

I could see Rodney and Ellen looking at me out of the corner of my eye, and I deliberately kept my gaze on Sarah, whose face was flush with indecision on how to answer Jeffers' question.

Finally, she nodded.

There was a silent exchange between Ellen and Rodney. Ellen, in particular, seemed to be having a hard time handling the revelation that Milla had come home and she hadn't known about it.

"I hadn't seen her since she left," Sarah said, lowering her eyes to her lap, where her fingers fidgeted nervously. "I'd heard shortly after she'd gone that she wasn't doing great. You know, like she was whacked out or whatever."

"And was she? When you saw her?" Jeffers asked.

Sarah shook her head. "She looked amazing."

"I'm so glad you're home. I know I probably should have called, but I was afraid if no one answered I'd take that as some kind of sign and then maybe I'd never have the nerve to come again so ... I've missed you so much, Sarah. And Rod and Ellen. Are they here? I want to talk to all of you."

"Milla, it's—"

"Been a long time. I know. And I know I said some horrible things when I left, and I'm not expecting you guys to forgive me right away. I want to earn your trust again. I'm hoping maybe we could..."

"What?"

"Try again. Take things slow."

"Do you honestly think you can come back here after all this time as if nothing's happened?"

"No. I'm going to make up for what I did. All of it. I'm—"

"How, Milla? How do you plan on doing that? Do you have any idea what Uncle Rod and Aunt Ellen went through after you left? Do you have any idea what it did to them? To me?"

"I'm sorry. I wasn't in a good place. I couldn't see that Rod only wanted to help me and I felt abandoned by you and I blamed—"

"Abandoned? Everything I did when we were growing up was for you. I protected you from the worst of it!"

"I know, Sarah. It's just that, at the time ... you and Ellen and—"

"'At the time,' Milla, you made everything about you. And you're doing it again now. Coming back here, thinking we'll all be so relieved to see you. That we'll just welcome

you with open arms and forget everything you put us through."

"No—"

"And it figures you'd come now. Right when we've just started to get our lives back. Right when we're happy again, as a family."

"Sarah, please. Please, just let me talk to them. Let me see them, at least. Let me—"

"Cameron arrived to pick me up and saw us arguing. I was relieved to see her, and I *did* want to welcome her back but ... I knew everything would change."

"What do you mean by 'everything'?" Lindsey asked.

"We'd become a family. Uncle Rod, Aunt Ellen, and me. And I was afraid. I knew how Milla could get, and I was afraid that we'd let her back in and things would be fine for a while but then they'd start fighting again and Aunt Ellen would cry again and Uncle Rod would blame himself and they didn't deserve that. We were finally happy."

"So, Cameron arrived while you two were arguing," Jeffers said. "What happened then?"

"Milla was more and more worked up. She was starting to cause a scene on the street. I was worried one of the neighbours would see her and mention something to Aunt Ellen or Uncle Rod. I was trying to quiet her down, but she wouldn't and then Cameron..."

"What did Cameron do, Sarah?"

"He ... injected her with something and she passed out. He told me it was just a sedative and that she'd be fine."

"Did you ask him why he just happened to have a sedative with him?"

Sarah shook her head. "I wasn't thinking clearly. Seeing Milla again completely threw me off balance and I knew

Ellen would be back soon so I just went with it. I needed to get her out of there before anyone came home."

"When did Cameron tell you about the basement?"

"Later that night. We'd been driving around for a while. Milla woke up and we argued again."

"Oh my god, what did you give me?"

"Be quiet."

"I've been clean, Sarah. For a year. I can't believe you drugged me."

"It was just a sedative. Relax. You needed to calm down. You were making a scene."

"Yeah, because you won't let me see my family."

"Your family? When have they ever been your family?"

"Sarah, I know I hurt them. I hurt you. But it's different now. I'm different now. I've gotten better. I just needed ... I don't know what. Some space, maybe. Time. But I have a boyfriend now and I just got a job, and we have a beautiful life and I've changed, Sarah. I've really changed. And I'm sorry. I'm so sorry."

"Oh, that's just great. While we've been beating ourselves up, destroying ourselves with worry over you, you were off having the time of your life. We were terrified that you were dead, but really you were living the high life."

"Sarah, that's not—"

"No, Milla, I'll tell you what's not. This. This is not going to happen. I will not let you waltz back into our lives. You are just like Dad and you are only thinking of yourself. You allowed us to suffer for years and now, because it's what you want, you think you can swoop in with your apologies and your boyfriend and whatever and everything will be hunky dory."

"Okay, fine. Maybe we can't go back to what we were. But you don't get to speak for Rod and Ellen."

"I am protecting them."

"LET ME OUT OF THIS VAN!"

"No. Not unless you promise you'll never try to see Uncle Rod and Aunt Ellen again."

"I'm not promising that. And you can't make me. I owe them an explanation and an apology. They deserve that."

"You only want to apologize to make yourself feel better. This has nothing to do with them."

"That's not true."

Silence.

"Sarah."

Silence.

"Sarah, let me out! What are you going to do? Keep me in here?"

She said she would come to the house everyday if that's what it took. I couldn't take that chance. I couldn't do that to Aunt Ellen and Uncle Rod. Not after everything they'd done for me. Cameron offered me a solution."

"I don't think you did it because of your aunt and uncle," Jeffers said.

"What are you talking about? I love them more than anything. Of course I did it for them."

"What about you?"

"What *about* me?"

"You spent your childhood taking care of your parents and your sister. Forced to when you were barely old enough to be able to. I think Milla coming back into your lives wasn't so much a threat to Rodney and Ellen's happiness as it was yours."

Sarah's back stiffened and she looked at Jeffers square on.

"Let's talk about the night Milla died," Lindsey said, trying to break the tension, trying to salvage the interview before Sarah refused to say anything more. "Milla went into labour early, didn't she? She wasn't due for a few more weeks, isn't that right?"

While Lindsey spoke, Sarah didn't take her eyes off Jeffers. But what was behind them changed. And by the time Lindsey had finished asking her question, Sarah sat hunched and defeated.

"Valerie called to tell me. I went down to see what was going on. There was a doctor and a nurse with her. And there was a lot of blood. She'd had some internal bleeding and they'd had to perform a C-section. The baby was in an incubator. It looked … like some kind of monster. They were trying to get the bleeding under control. I told the doctor and nurse to leave."

"Sarah, we can't leave. She's hemorrhaging. If we don't act fast, she'll—"

"Get out of here now. Both of you."

"Sarah…"

"You take orders from Val, Cameron, and me. No one else. And I'm telling you to leave."

"We can save her if—"

"Would you rather I tell you you're fired? Because I don't know how you'll ever be able to cover your son's treatments without this little moonlighting gig of yours. Or you, doctor, how will you support your habit then?"

"Sarah, please."

"Leave her. Leave the baby. And get out of here now or you're done."

"I did regret it, you know," Sarah said to Jeffers.

"Letting your sister die?"

"All of it. But there was no way Cameron would let her go after what she'd been through. After what she knew. There was no way he'd let either of us go. So, yes, I let her die because it was the only way I could free her."

"What happened after the doctor and nurse left?"

"I put her and the baby in one of Cameron's old hockey bags and drove them out of town. I didn't have a plan really. I just drove. And before I knew it, I was outside the drive-in.

"One of the only happy memories I have with my parents was when they took us to see *Beauty and the Beast* there. It was during one of their good times. When they were well. My Dad had borrowed a car from one of his friends. It was a special showing and it was packed. Milla and I loved it. We sang the songs for months afterward. I thought it was a fitting resting place."

Sarah stopped speaking. Jeffers made a small gesture to Lindsey to turn off the camera.

"It's over?" Rodney Koepper asked.

"We'll continue a little later," Crayne said. "We have more questions, but this is a good time for a break. Why don't you and your wife get something to eat? I'll call when we're going to start up again."

Ellen shook her head, but it was Rodney who answered.

"Neither of us has an appetite. Is there somewhere my wife could lie down?"

"Of course. Follow me."

"I can't imagine what a shock this must be for them," I said to Morris, who nodded thoughtfully. I wondered how much still managed to shock him in this line of work.

"You should go home and rest," he said. "Most of the questions remaining for Sarah are about the operation. Nothing Detective Jeffers can't fill you in on later."

"Yes, sir," I said, hearing Emma Samuel in my voice.

"And Miss James, we will have a proper debrief when you've fully recovered, but I want to thank you for everything you've done."

"It was a pleasure to be of service, sir."

He slipped out of the room just as he had entered.

I heard a muffled conversation outside the door and moments later, Jeffers entered.

"Morris wants you to go home."

"I know. I'm going," I said, getting to my feet. "There's just one thing I hope we can do first."

Chapter 29

Cameron was sitting in a holding cell. He hadn't yet been transferred to a more permanent facility where he'd wait out his sentencing.

"I already told you everything," he said when Jeffers and I entered.

"Not everything," Jeffers corrected. He held a photo of Laura in front of Cameron's face. "How did you come by her?"

"She was messed up."

"That's not what I asked."

"Is this going to get me more time?"

"With the amount you're going to get, would it even matter?"

Cameron snickered and turned his face away from us.

"I can tell you one thing," Jeffers said. "Cooperation goes a long way in cases like this. Might not affect the years you get, but it could have a hand in which one of our fine penitentiaries you end up in."

Cameron bristled at this. "Fine. She was in the wrong place at the wrong time."

"What do you mean?" I asked.

"I was down at the gorge getting rid of … one of them…"

"Bernadelle."

"Sure. And that one," he said, pointing to Laura's picture, "came out of nowhere. Scared the life out of me. She saw what I was doing. She said she didn't care, that she wouldn't tell anyone, but, you know, I couldn't take the chance. Besides, she was a good age. In good shape."

Jeffers looked at me and raised an eyebrow as if asking if I'd gotten what I needed.

I raised a finger, indicating I had one more question.

"Was she pregnant when you took her?"

"What did Paul say when you told him?" Natalie asked over the phone later that night.

"He was relieved to hear she hadn't been pregnant. It was important for him to hear the rest too. Doesn't make it any easier, though."

"How could it? My god. I can't even imagine."

"He's so broken," I said. "I've never seen him like this. I don't know what to do."

"I don't think there's a rule book for a situation like this. Just give him time."

"Yeah."

"And don't push. You know how much you hated that after your parents died."

"So true."

"Listen, we can talk more about this when you're feeling better. I know you need to rest."

"Thanks."

"Do you need anything? Do you need me to come?"

"I'm okay."

I had gone to the theatre, at the insistence of the powers that be, to be fitted for a microphone for the evening performance of *Arms and the Man* even though I was rather emphatic that my understudy go on. My understudy, Aislinn, was a very eager—maybe too eager—but extremely hardworking member of the Emerging Artists Program, which, in addition to giving young actors the prestige of being part of the company, provides them with mentorship support, training, and performance experience.

I had lobbied heavily for the experience factor as I knew her roles that season were mostly non-speaking townspeople and maids. And although I knew she was not entirely right for Louka, she would be fine for one night, and the experience would be one she would never forget.

In the end, my director for *Quality Street* barrelled into the proceedings and said that if I didn't get the rest I needed now, I might miss more performances in the future, so the microphone idea was dropped, and I was sent home.

I was sure it wasn't just my own well-being he'd been thinking about. My name was one of the things drawing audiences to an otherwise unknown play, and he was enjoying the success. But whatever the case, I was grateful to be home with my feet up and Moustache acting as my nursemaid.

The police had found my phone in Cameron's van. It had been overrun with texts from Adam wondering when I'd be arriving at the party, giving me hell for not being at the party, and then apologizing for giving me hell when he'd heard what had happened. He had been quite distraught, if I had interpreted his emojis correctly.

We had spoken, briefly, and I had promised him that I was fine and that I'd be at the wedding in a couple of days. But after my appearance at the theatre, a game of telephone had evidently been played in which my condition had moved from stable to severe and was currently teetering on the edge of critical and he was texting every second he had the chance.

Jarod Riley had been sending me texts after every scene to let me know how Aislinn had done, how much he missed me, and wondering what I needed and what he could do.

Between Adam and Jarod, my phone had been dinging all evening, in spite of the fact that both men were in the middle of performances and insistent that I rest.

I turned my phone to silent and considered the small pile of mail I had discarded on the coffee table. I opened the top envelope and pulled out the two tickets I had ordered for a day cruise aboard one of the tall ships. The tour was scheduled for two weeks from now. So much had happened since the time I thought it would be such a nice surprise. Now I wasn't so sure.

I leaned my head back and yawned deeply, surprising myself that it didn't result in a fit of coughing. Moustache was nestled in the crook of my arm. He lifted his head from where it lay on my chest and all but stuck his entire snout in my mouth, examining it for signs of concern. Satisfied that all was well, he dropped his head back into position and resumed monitoring my breathing.

Paul came in moments later and kissed my forehead.

"I'm not asleep," I said.

"You should be. But I'm glad you're not. How are you feeling?"

"Much better actually," I said and took a deep breath to show him.

He sat down on the floor and leaned his back against the couch. I ran my fingers through his hair. He took my hand, kissed it, and then held it to his chest.

"I'm sorry I haven't been here for you," he said.

"And I'm sorry I haven't been there for you. How was Laura today? Any improvement?"

Paul shook his head. "Her parents arrived. They're going to take her back to Ottawa as soon as she's released, which should be soon. Physically, she's mostly fine. Surprisingly. But mentally ... I don't know. She doesn't recognize me or her parents ... it's like she's retreated so deeply within herself that she isn't a part of this world."

"Maybe that's what she had to do to survive."

"This is going to sound horrible, but I can't help but think it would have been better if Cameron had just killed her that day at the gorge. That's why she'd gone there. She didn't want to live anymore and to be stuck living like this…"

"I don't think that sounds horrible. She's suffering. She was suffering before and wherever this place is now that she's created for herself, she's suffering still. You just want that suffering to end. That's not a horrible wish at all."

He held my hand tighter then shifted on his hip so he could look at me.

His face was drawn. The light behind his eyes had dimmed, but I could still see a flicker and knew it would come back in time.

"I love you so much," he said.

"I love you all the much."

He brought his hand to my face, and I leaned into the cool metal of the ring he still wore, never taking my eyes off his.

A moment passed between us. Something understood but unsaid that lingered in the quiet that surrounded us.

Chapter 30

There was so much noise in the small room that had been designated as Adam's dressing area.

Niagara-on-the-Lake was an incredibly popular wedding destination with venues booked years in advance. With only a few weeks between the wedding announcement and the event itself, Powell's ex-military father had called in a handful of favours and had managed to secure the grounds of Butler's Barracks for his son's big day.

For over one hundred and fifty years, the Barracks had borne witness to military activity as Canada evolved from a British colony to a nation in its own right, and was considered a National Historic Site. There were five original structures still in existence on the property and a couple of rooms had been made available to the wedding party in what had once been the Junior Commissariat Officer's Quarters.

Adam looked radiant and my heart swelled seeing him so happy.

But that radiance manifested itself in some very big jubilation in a very small space, and I excused myself from the excitement and stepped into the waning light of the day behind the building and savoured a moment of tranquility.

"You solo tonight?"

I turned and saw Jarod Riley coming around the building toward me.

I wondered if he'd planted a tracking device on my person without my knowledge.

"No," I said. "Paul's meeting me. He got tied up at the clinic."

Monday is usually the dark day in the theatre—the one official day off—but a workday for most of the population, vets included.

"You sound almost like your old self. That's good to hear," Jarod said.

I'd only missed the one performance of *Arms and the Man*. I found *Quality Street* to be much more of a significant vocal strain given that Phoebe has so many more lines than Louka, but I had managed to get through all of my performances.

I hadn't given Jarod too many details other than that I had escaped a fire, but the timing and the lack of other fires in the area made it pretty easy to deduce which blaze I had been in. One by one, the other women had been released and reunited with their loved ones, and the families of the women who had died had been making statements. The news stations and papers had been featuring the story heavily for a few days now, so I was sure he had questions about what really happened.

Adam and Powell's wedding was neither the time nor the place for answers, so I changed the course of the conversation to the tents that were set up on the grass. All the tables and chairs, flowers, and strings of lights were very tasteful and quite simple, and we both laughed as we imagined the intense negotiations that must have played out between the grooms given Adam's penchant for all things flamboyant. We were both hedging guesses as to what Powell had had to sacrifice in order to walk away with such a big win when Paul's car pulled into the small parking lot.

I smiled and waved.

Jarod's face registered a fleeting moment of disappointment before lighting up with a winning smile. "Your knight arrives at last."

"Why aren't you dressed?" I asked as Paul approached.

Paul was still in his work clothes. He looked to Jarod. A silent appeal for privacy.

"I'm going to get myself another drink," Jarod said. "Can I get you two anything?"

"We're fine," I said.

"Thanks, man," Paul said, and Jarod rounded the corner out of sight.

"Um..." I said, noticing Paul had yet to make eye contact with me since he'd arrived.

When he did, I felt the floor drop out of my stomach.

"I can't stay," he said.

"Oh, okay. Did something happen at work or...?"

"I don't just mean for the wedding."

"I don't under—"

"I need to say this and I ... please don't speak ... I need to..."

"Paul?"

"They released Laura today. Her parents found a place for her in a long-term care home and … and…"

"You knew that was—"

"Shh, please. I need…" He started pacing, wringing his hands slightly. "I need to go … there. I need to help her get settled. I need to … oh god, Bells, I'm so sorry. I can't explain it. I can't explain why, but I need to be there with her."

"Bella," Jarod said, popping his head around the side of the building, "they're starting soon."

I fixed a smile to my face and nodded, unable to speak.

Jarod lingered briefly, looking from Paul to me before returning the way he'd come.

"What's that sound?" I asked as a screeching filled the air.

"Brimstone. He's in his carrier."

I looked to the car and saw it had been packed.

"You're going now?" I asked in surprise.

He looked at me with tears in his eyes.

"Bells, ever since I saw her in the hospital, I've been feeling so much shame. It's consumed me. It's all I can think about. I got her note and I … didn't look for her, I didn't call it in, I didn't do anything. I was so angry with her for doing that again. For putting me through that again. For losing her again. I was so focused on what her death did to me. Selfish. I was so selfish. And if I hadn't been, maybe … She's been in that place because of me. Because of my inaction. I failed her. And I know I can't fix it—fix her—but I don't deserve to be here, loved by you, when she's … I'm sorry. I'm so sorry."

His green eyes shone with tears that streamed down his cheeks.

We stared at each other, neither of us knowing what to say. Me in shock, him crumbling before my very eyes.

I reached for him, but he put his arm out to stop me.

"Don't," he said. "I won't be able to let go. And I have to … let go."

"Bella!" Adam's voice rang out.

I turned toward the sound and when I looked back, Paul was walking to his car.

I willed my legs to run, my voice to cry out, but could do neither.

Paul didn't look back. Not once he got to the car. Not once he started the ignition. Not once he drove away. Not once.

"Bella!" Adam called again.

"Bella," Jarod said, coming around the corner, "we're starting. And Adam needs help with his train."

I looked at him, barely registering what he had said.

"Is everything all right? Where's—"

"Yeah, everything's … yeah," I said, my heart breaking apart beneath my party dress. "I'm coming."

In Gratitude

First of all, I know you hate me for that ending. It pained me to write it. My vision for this series has always been five books, and I've known how this one would end for a while now. I've had longer to come to terms with the ending and, in time, I hope you will let it excite you for book four. In the meantime, feel free to hate me a little longer. 😊

I discovered the game Plants vs. Zombies shortly after I started writing this book. It's a miracle I finished it. And I certainly wouldn't have without the help of some amazing people.

My dear friends and one-time neighbours, Peter Millard and Gabrielle Jones, are my Niagara-on-the-Lake and Shaw Festival experts. They have been on the receiving end of many a phone call, and I have only been able to stay current with ever-changing details of the beautiful town I once called home and get some real insider knowledge of the Festival because of them.

Another friend and one-time neighbour—well, if living down the hall in a university dorm constitutes a neighbour—is Chris Lamont. He is a registered herbalist and fielded all my questions with enthusiasm. He does some amazing things. Check him out at http://christheherbalist.com or on Facebook at @christheherbalist.

Rhona Buchan and Harold Murphy were kind enough to offer their legal expertise. Should I ever need a lawyer, I'd be lucky to have either of them work on my behalf.

I was also fortunate to have been able to pick the brains of firefighters Rolyn Potter and Nicholas Aiden and, especially, retired Fire Chief Donald Laffoley.

I want to thank Sharon King-Campbell for getting me into some hard to reach, classified areas; my book club—Michelle, Sarah, Kelly, and Colleen—my mother, and my Auntie Mame for trudging through the first draft and offering some invaluable insight; my Aunt Barbara, who has been my draft two reader since I started this series; George Robertson for providing the final, critical eye; and a certain Sergeant with the RCMP, who is always eager to help and seems genuinely tickled by all the stuff I get Bella and Jeffers into.

I was able to get the incredible Ruth Dwight on board again to design the cover, much to my absolute delight, and I was blessed with the best editor I could ever imagine, Mary Ann Blair. The way she is able to sift through my errors, over-written sentences, and bad habits and tap into my thoughts and the world I have created is nothing short of amazing. I am ever, ever grateful to her.

A Bernedoodle named Sebastian came into my life not long after I lost Grady, and he is the happiest dog I have ever known. He keeps me smiling and laughing, and it didn't take long for some of him to rub off on Moustache.

As ever, my mom and dad have remained my biggest fans and staunchest supporters. I am so thankful for their love and return it wholeheartedly.

And I am so thankful for you. If you hadn't gotten invested in this series, I'd still be fighting the zombies.

About the Author

Alexis is a Canadian actor and author. She lives in St. John's, Newfoundland and Labrador with her Bernedoodle, Sebastian.